TREASURE OF GREY MANOR

He hurried out into the quiet night. The rain had stopped and the air smelled fresh after the staleness of Grey Manor. A half moon was gliding out of the clouds and glimmering on the wet cobbles of Manor Walk, and by its light Jamie could see that the phonebox was occupied. Three youths. A small one, a tall thin one and a square, heavy one. He slid into the shadow of Grey Manor gates and waited. A minute later Eric Gott stepped out with his two friends. A light wind carried snatches of their words to Jamie's ears: ". . . doesn't get it tomorrow . . . steal it . . . ten quid *each*!" And then they were gone.

Other titles in the Mystery Thriller series include:

The Song of The Dead by Anthony Masters
The Ferryman's Son by Ian Strachan

TREASURE OF GREY MANOR

by
TERRY DEARY
Illustrated by Alan Fraser

Hippo Books
Scholastic Publications Limited
London

Scholastic Publications Ltd.,
10 Earlham Street, London WC2H 9RX, UK

Scholastic Inc.,
730 Broadway, New York, NY 10003, USA

Scholastic Tab Publications Ltd.,
123 Newkirk Road, Richmond Hill,
Ontario L4C 3G5, Canada

Ashton Scholastic Pty Ltd.,
P O Box 579, Gosford, New South Wales,
Australia

Ashton Scholastic Ltd.,
165 Marua Road, Panmure, Auckland 6,
New Zealand

First published by Scholastic Publications Ltd., 1990

ISBN 0 590 76319 9

Typeset by AKM Associates (UK) Ltd., Southall, London
Printed by Cox & Wyman Ltd., Reading, Berks

AUTHOR'S NOTE

My thanks to the following for help with this book:-
Jack Bainbridge *of Berwick for the information on body-snatching.* **Alton Pickersgill** *of Sunderland for background on the Sunderland Cholera epidemic of 1831.* **Hilary Williams** *of Boldon for research on 1830's costume.* **Marie Young, John Mason and the pupils of Hetton School** *for developing the characters in the 'River Wear Drama Enterprise, 1988.'*

The characters in this book are imaginary, but the historical backdrop was drawn from a real cholera epidemic in Sunderland in 1831. The book is dedicated to the memory of those who died.

Chapter One

He was sixteen. So was she.

He went to Seawell Comprehensive school; a bleak collection of concrete and glass blocks overlooking the bleaker North Sea. So did she.

But that was about all they had in common.

His face was plain and good-natured, topped with an unkempt mop of sandy hair. She had immaculately groomed black hair over a coolly beautiful face.

His eyes were a muddy mix of brown and green. Hers were clear and blue as deep as velvet.

They'd shared lessons for the past five years but she'd never spoken to him. Too much of a snob, the boys reckoned. Until today, that is.

Now he found himself standing at her front door, searching for the courage to push the doorbell. An impressive front door from a distance – he'd looked at it for five minutes through the gateway in the thick, dark hedge. But here, close to, it was weathered and shabby, maroon paint peeling in places to reveal a coat of grey beneath. Grey as its name, Grey Manor.

He licked his dry lips and jabbed a shaking finger at the white enamel button. He gave a nervous laugh when it failed to move.

The boy huddled into his anorak. "I tried," he muttered to himself. "I can say I called – say I rang the bell but got no answer. It's not my fault if the bell doesn't work."

The thought brought a thin smile to his face. He gave a sharp nod and began to back away from the door. Back towards the black iron gate. Back to the road and then back to the warm safety of his own kitchen. He didn't get five steps.

"Can I help you?" the man asked.

He had come as silently as the October mist that swirled along the cobbled street behind him. His suit was black, shiny at the elbows and dusty on the rounded shoulders. The man's face was pale and worn with deep, dark lines of care. Thin, colourless hair lay limply on his bent head.

"Mr Grey?" the boy began.

"Can I help you?" the man repeated flatly. He advanced down the path, pushing the damp weeds aside with his rolled black umbrella. "What do you want?" His eyes were red-rimmed, glaring, suspicious.

The boy tried a weak smile. "I'm in the same class

as Trish, your daughter," he explained. "She's a . . . a friend. At least I go to Seawell Comprehensive with her."

The man snorted. "Ha! That's no recommendation! Seawell Comprehensive produces some very undesirable sorts!"

"I'm Jamie. Jamie Williams. Trish invited me to come round this evening," the boy went on.

Mr Grey rummaged in his frayed briefcase and pulled out a bunch of keys. Pushing past the nervous boy he fitted a key into the crimson door and opened it. "I'll tell my daughter she has a visitor," he muttered, stepping inside. Jamie made to follow him but the door swung firmly shut in his face. He leaned against a doorpost and huddled deeper into his anorak. Fingers of mist groped their way into the overgrown garden and somewhere a foghorn gave a mournful blast. The mist was drifting over the high garden wall and twisting itself into soft shapes.

Jamie shuddered. He knew what was on the other side of the wall. He'd had to walk past it on his way to Grey Manor. It was the town's old graveyard. Full of crooked, mossy headstones, it was unused now, yet something had made him nervous as he hurried past in the growing gloom. Had he imagined some slight sound? Or perhaps the faintest movement had caught the corner of his eye. He hadn't waited to investigate.

And now the sea mist was drifting over the wall towards him, as if the thing in the graveyard was following him to see what he was up to. So it wasn't surprising that he jumped when the door swung open behind him and the weak hall light spilled on to the steps. "Hello, Jamie," she said. Her dark blue eyes examined him sharply. "You seem nervous."

He forced a weak grin. "No, no!" he lied and dropped his eyes from her searching look. There was something different about her that unsettled him. He'd never seen her dressed in anything other than her school uniform before now, and now she wore jeans with a blue velvet top that perfectly matched her eyes. But that wasn't the difference. It was that she seemed older, more in control, and that disturbed him. Her cool gaze seemed to be summing him up – giving him marks out of ten.

She held the door open wider as if inviting him in, then called down the dim passageway. "We'll go to the library, Father!"

Jamie had understood that they'd be working in her house. "Oh! The library will be closed by the time we get there!"

The girl turned back and looked at him uncertainly. "The library in our house," she explained. "We have a library here, you know."

"Of course," Jamie muttered and followed her as she walked down the hall. He'd started badly. That was another mark off her mental score for him, he reckoned.

He closed the door. The hall light was weak and the manor as bleak and cold inside as outside. Dark, wooden-panelled walls held gloomy portraits of gloomier old men. A wide staircase led up into the darkness. Trish led him along a passage to the left, over a carpet so thin that their footsteps echoed off the boards beneath.

At the end of the first passage he stopped and stared at the portrait that faced him.

"What's wrong?" Trish asked.

He pointed to the portrait. "That girl . . . the long black hair . . . the deep blue eyes. She looks so much like you. But the clothes – that dark blue dress is too old-fashioned."

Trish looked embarrassed. "Other people have said she looks like me," she admitted. "It's a girl called Marie Grey. Actually, she's the one we're doing the project on. Funny you should notice the portrait."

"She's beautiful," Jamie murmured, tearing his eyes away from the picture to follow Trish. The eyes of the portrait followed him.

The girl reached an oak door and turned. "It's warmer in the library," she said. "I've put the fire on."

"Good," Jamie said. A stupid, pointless remark but he was feeling more and more uneasy.

At least the library lived up to his idea of how Grey Manor would be. Shelves from floor to ceiling were lined with leather-bound books. The fire blazed warmly enough but couldn't fill the huge fireplace. Trish followed Jamie's gaze. "It's hard to keep an old place like this warm in winter," she explained. "Not unless you're rich."

"And you're not?" he almost said, clumsy in his nervousness, but he didn't want to lose any more points in Trish's eyes so instead he muttered, "Yeah. It must be hard."

She nodded to a leather-topped table in the centre of the room. "Have a seat and take your coat off."

Jamie shrugged himself out of his anorak and handed it to Trish. She dropped it on to one of the armchairs by the fireplace and walked across to the window. She pulled heavy curtains across and shut out the dank evening. The crackling fire added a warm light to the small lamp on the table but couldn't reach the furthest corners of the room.

Trish ran her fingers along a row of books. "Ah, here it is," she muttered, pulling one out. She placed the book carefully on the table and sat next to Jamie.

She gave him her hard stare again. This time he managed to hold her gaze while she found the right words. "You know why I asked you to come round here to work on this project with me?"

He shrugged. "Mr Waites wants us to do a project for GCSE History. Wants us to see what he calls 'original sources' – old documents, books, photographs, artefacts and so on. He said we could work with friends."

"But I haven't any friends," the girl said.

"The other girls . . ."

"Don't much like me. They speak to me. They're polite, but they don't *like* me. They're not . . . friends. So I chose you. Don't you want to know why?" she asked intently.

His mouth opened and closed while he seached for the answer. He didn't have an answer. He'd been as

6

shocked as the rest of the class when Trish had announced quietly, "I'll work with Jamie Williams, sir."

Of course the lads on the football team had had an answer. "She fancies you, Jamie!" they'd jeered next lesson as they changed for games.

"You'll be all right there, son! Get well in with her! You should see the house she lives in!" Alan Oliver had cried.

"Nah, she's a snobby bitch," Mark Young had put in quietly. "Too good for our Jamie. She must want something off him."

"Well, it's not his weedy body!" Alan scoffed and flicked at Jamie with his towel.

Jamie had laughed with the rest of them. But all the same he wondered. "I suppose you thought I could help you with the project," he said.

She shook her head impatiently. "Why *you*? Why not Sharon Walker or Helen Teasdale?"

He shook his head uncomfortably. "I don't know!" he admitted. "Why me?"

The girl took a deep breath. "I want to pass this exam. I need to get to university. History isn't my best subject. You got the top mark last time we did an assignment like this. I want to use you to get me a top mark this time."

Jamie nodded slowly. "OK," he said.

Trish blinked. "OK? Is that all you can say?"

He felt uncomfortable. It was what he expected. What did she want him to say? "Yeah . . . OK!"

She sat back a little and looked down her straight

nose at him. He felt she was disappointed. Knocked yet another mark off his rating. "You don't mind being . . . used like that?"

He gave a shy smile and looked up at her. "We don't have a library in our house. We don't have a room full of 'original sources'. You do. Maybe I'm using you," he said.

The girl thought about this for a moment, frowning till her dark eyebrows made a straight line over her worried eyes. And suddenly she smiled for the first time since Jamie had known her. "You're right," she said. "When you put it like that it does seem a good deal."

Jamie smiled back. At last he'd scored a point in his favour. "I'd have helped you anyway, even if you hadn't had a room full of books," he said.

She shook her head. "I know, but I wouldn't have been happy. Most of the boys in the class think I'm a snob anyway."

"They don't!" Jamie tried to protest, but she went on.

"But I'm not! They never gave me a chance. It's because I live in this dump they think we're posh."

"It's not a dump!" Jamie tried again to interrupt.

"Oh, it is!" she moaned. "You know my mother moved out two years ago because she couldn't stand it any more. All she wanted was a small modern house at Whitley, easy to keep warm and clean. But Dad wouldn't sell Grey Manor."

"Why not?" Jamie asked quietly.

The girl shrugged angrily. "You'd know if you

knew my father. He's got a thing about the history of the Grey family in Seawell. Lived here for three centuries and all that."

"I can understand that," Jamie said.

"Then he has this obsession with . . ." she began and stopped suddenly.

"With what?" Jamie asked.

"It's stupid."

"With what?" the boy urged.

"With . . . the fortune that the Grey family owned. What Dad calls their treasure," she muttered unhappily. "He thinks that if he can find out what happened to their wealth he can afford to live here like a lord, and maybe my mother would come back."

"Do you think there's any treasure here?" Jamie asked.

"Not *here*," Trish said carefully. "Not in this house. It couldn't be. Dad's searched every inch. That was one of the things that drove my mother out – that and the time he spent in here looking through the old books for a clue."

"But you do believe there's a Grey family treasure somewhere?"

The girl ran a pale hand through her fine hair and chose her words carefully. "There is a fortune which has never been accounted for. Joshua Grey made it in the coal and shipping trade. It was there in the family accounts in 1830. Gold and silver plates at the dinner table, jewellery and dresses for Mrs Grey and her daughters worth a fortune! But when Joshua Grey died in 1835 there was no trace of it. My father's seen his will – all he left was Grey Manor. Even the coal business and the shipping business had been sold. But there's no record of what he did with the money they raised."

"And since then?" Jamie asked.

"Since then the Grey family, right down to Father, have had the Manor but never enough money to run it properly."

"Perhaps . . ." Jamie began. The door swung open. Jamie turned. The table lamp lit Mr Grey's lined face from a low angle and made it look harsher than usual.

"Not finished yet, Trish?" he asked. "There's too much coal on that fire. Waste not, want not," he added.

"Sorry, Father," the girl said, clearly embarrassed. She rose to her feet. "Come along, Jamie. This will give you something to start on. Maybe we can talk about it tomorrow in the lesson." She pushed the book across the table towards him.

Mr Grey moved swiftly and snatched it up. "What book's that?" he said.

"It's the diary of Marie Grey, Father. Jamie and I are doing a humanities project. I thought we could look at life in the 1830s from the point of view of a girl of our age."

Mr Grey slid a pair of spectacles from the top pocket of his dusty jacket and squinted at the first page. "Hah!" he snorted. "Worthless. This isn't real history, just foolish female tittle-tattle. It's written in some childish code. I spent hours working it out, then

10

I read the first two pages and discovered it's nonsense about clothes and local gossip."

"I think that's the sort of detail Mr Waites wants us to discover," Jamie put in. "The everyday things of life then are more interesting than the wars and the politics."

Mr Grey turned on him with a sour sneer. "That's what they teach you in History these days, is it? Wish I'd been able to send you to a good private school, girl!"

"Seawell Comprehensive has the best History department in the region," Jamie argued.

The man's lip curled upwards. "Get many university graduates from Seawell, do they?" he asked.

"Time you were going, Jamie!" Trish cut in quickly, warning.

But it was too late. "Yes," Jamie replied, his face pale and angry. "My older brother, Robert, not only got a degree but he's lecturing at Durham University in History, and *he* went to Seawell Comprehensive!"

The man stepped back as sharply as if Jamie had punched him. His jaw sagged, but his eyes showed his mind was working frantically. "Robert . . . Robert . . . what's your name again? Surname?"

"Williams," Jamie said. He felt uncomfortable. He could sense Trish's tension as she stood by him.

"Hah!" the man laughed. "I might have guessed. Robert Williams. I've read some of his articles in the local history magazine. He's some sort of communist, isn't he?"

It was Jamie's turn to be taken aback. "Well, he's a bit left-wing . . ." he admitted.

"A bit!" Mr Grey screeched. "Everything he writes he tries to prove that the poor workers were trodden into the ground by the big bad businessmen. Men like the Grey family. Isn't that so?"

"Well . . ."

The man advanced menacingly towards Jamie. "Well, you tell your brother that if it hadn't been for the Greys and families like them there wouldn't even *be* a Seawell town."

The man's eyes glowed hotly in the red light of the fire. He licked at the flecks of spittle that came to his lips and his voice dropped to a harsh croak. "Father . . ." Trish moaned, frightened and embarrassed. He ignored her.

"The Greys, the Fawcetts and the Macmillans built Seawell town. They risked their money to fetch the coal from the ground and ship it down to London. And if the workers had to work long and hard for poor wages then it was sad, but it was a hard life. And if the Greys and the Fawcetts and the Macmillans made their fortunes then it might seem a bit unfair to the likes of your communist brother. But it doesn't make my ancestors cruel criminals. Even if the Grey family were monsters then the likes of you have had your vengeance now. With your taxes and your death duties you've clawed our money back. You've left us poor, and what have you done with our money? You've dished out free education for all. Built monstrosities like Seawell Comprehensive school.

12

Taught people like you to despise the beauty of Grey Manor!"

Mr Grey's eyes were bulging. He panted for breath and the only other sounds were the crackling of the fire and the drone of the foghorn. He picked up the old leather book from the table and waved it under Jamie's nose. "But when you want to look into the past, when you need proof of the way we lived our heartless lives, then you come crawling back to us to beg us for our books."

"It was my idea, Father," Trish said quickly.

"Well, you're welcome to the book," the man said, pushing it hard into Jamie's stomach. "Take it. Show your brother that we Greys know how to look after the past. You despise us for clinging on to the past, and you certainly don't pay us to preserve the past, but we give it you freely. Take it!" He jabbed the book at the boy again until Jamie grasped it. "And now get out!"

Chapter Two

Trish stood beside Jamie on the worn front step of Grey Manor. After an awkward silence she murmured, "Sorry. Father has this thing about money. That's why he's so keen to find the treasure."

"Maybe my brother could help," Jamie said.

The girl drew her breath in sharply. Her eyes widened. "Don't ever suggest that to Father! He'd rather die in poverty than find the family fortune with the help of someone like your brother!"

Jamie sighed. "Of course. Sorry. It was stupid of me to suggest it." The awkward silence fell again.

The fog was so thick now that even the street lamp was just a faint amber glow beyond the dark silhouette of the graveyard wall. Trish shivered. "Sorry," Jamie said again. "I'm keeping you out here in the cold. You go inside." She nodded, but didn't move.

"Will you have a chance to read the diary tonight?" she asked.

He turned slightly away from her. "Trish . . ." he began.

"Yes?" she waited. "Go on, say it!"

"I . . . that top History grade . . . I . . . I mean . . . it wasn't exactly because I'm great at History. I mean," he put in quickly, "I'm interested but not that good."

"You can't be any worse than me," she said with an encouraging smile. "I really would like your help. Two heads are better than one, even two thick heads!"

"What I meant to say was . . ."

"Your brother helped you," she finished for him.

He looked round quickly and found her smiling an understanding smile. "You guessed?"

She shrugged. "Everyone in the class guessed."

"Mr Waites never suspected . . ."

Trish threw her head back and laughed. "Of course he did!"

Jamie winced at the shame of the thought. "He gave me top marks."

"That's what the Humanities course is all about. Being resourceful, finding out by asking people who know. Your brother didn't do the essay for you, did he?"

"No, but I talked to him about it," Jamie admitted.

"And that's exactly what anyone in the class could have done – I mean, talked to the librarians or museum people. That's what they're there for. I could have asked my father for help; he's a keen historian. I could have asked for his help on this project. Local history – that's right up his street," Trish said.

Jamie thought for a moment. "Why didn't you?"

Trish shook her head and he noticed the way the careful cut made the dark hair fall straight back into place. "He wouldn't have understood. He's old-fashioned – thinks it's cheating. He's a bit like you really!"

Jamie opened his mouth to protest then realised she was having a joke at his expense. He smiled at her and felt a sudden warmth shared in the chill of the October fog.

"I'll take this diary round to Robert's house now," he said. "If it's in code I'll need his help."

"You're going to Durham at this time of night?" Trish asked, surprised.

"No. Robert lives in Seawell. Commutes to the university every day. It's only fifteen miles."

"Ah," Trish said and gazed into the darkness, a slight frown clouding her face.

"Something wrong?" the boy asked, following her gaze towards the graveyard wall.

"I thought I heard something . . . something over the wall," she explained.

"Joshua Grey turning in his grave at the thought of what we're doing with his books!" Jamie joked. But Trish didn't smile.

"No. There are no such things as ghosts. But . . .

but I do keep hearing things in that graveyard lately. My bedroom overlooks it, you know."

Jamie was about to tell her that he thought he'd heard something on his way to Grey Manor, but sensed her fear and didn't want to add to it. "Probably stray cats chasing mice," he said.

She smiled at him, grateful for the reassurance. "Probably," she agreed.

Still she seemed to be straining her ears and edging closer to the comfort of the shabby front door. "I'll get along to Robert's house, then," Jamie said briskly and set off down the dark path. He reached the gate and turned. She was silhouetted against the weak hall light and looked vulnerable.

"Thanks, Jamie!" she called and waved. "Thanks for your help!"

He waved back and watched her close the door and then even that feeble light was gone. The thick hedge along the front of Grey Manor seemed to hold a hundred pairs of eyes that watched his progress. He tried to whistle but his mouth was dry and only a weak, tuneless squeak came out.

After a dozen or so quick strides he came to the rusting railings that ran along the front of the graveyard and edged away from them. He wanted to run, then felt ashamed. Trish lived next door to this place. She said there were no such things as ghosts. If she wasn't afraid then he sure as hell wasn't. But when the first sound came out of the graveyard his stomach lurched. A few whispered words and a muffled laugh.

Then, suddenly, the glint of metal in the weak amber glow of the street lamp. He ducked instinctively and gasped. The metal object fell in the gutter with a hollow clatter – an empty beer can.

Jamie blew out a long breath. At least some drunken lunatic was better than a ghost. He kicked the can angrily and it disappeared into the darkness. He strode on, followed by the laughter and a scuttering of feet beyond the fence. Muffled words and then, quite clearly, a mocking, "Thanks, Jamie . . . thanks for your help!"

Whoever was in the graveyard had heard Trish's farewell call. And what else had they overheard?

"Thanks, Jamie!" came the voice again.

Then a second, deeper voice chimed in. "Give us a kiss, Jamie!" Jamie's fear turned to anger. Then he realised that was what they wanted.

He bit back an angry reply and called, "Come out here and I'll give you more than a kiss!"

He'd reached the wide entrance now and he waited. Out of the fog loomed three shadows, unsteady on their drunken feet but menacing none the less. "Oh yeah, Williams?" said the short one in the middle. "What will you give us?" And then Jamie recognised him. Eric Gott. The laziest and most troublesome boy at Seawell Comprehensive. Jamie had been bullied by Gott and his gang of hangers-on in the third and fourth years. But as Jamie had adopted a crowd of friends from the football team and Gott's friends had left the school early, the Gott gang had left Jamie alone to seek softer targets among the younger pupils.

Now, as the three walked towards Jamie, he was relieved to find that the old fear had gone. He faced them calmly. "Hello, Shorty," he nodded to Christopher Short – ironically nicknamed because he was so tall and spindly. "Hello, Podge," he said to David Hodge, the thick-set boy on Gott's right. He deliberately left the leader till last. "Hello, Eric," he said.

Eric Gott's eyes narrowed. "Not Eric – Rick. Call me Rick."

"Sorry . . . Eric," Jamie smiled, "I'll try to remember."

"You do that, Williams," he said, waving a half-full beer can under Jamie's nose. His long brown hair was usually greasy but now the damp of the fog made it hang in ugly rat's tails around his thin face.

Jamie nodded towards the graveyard. "Isn't it trespassing, being in there?" he asked. "I wouldn't want to see you in court again, Eric."

"Nah," Gott sneered. "Visiting me granny's grave, wasn't I, lads?" he said and his two partners giggled.

"Yeah, Rick. Decorating it with fresh cans!" lanky Short put in.

Jamie shrugged. "Must have a very old granny. No one's been buried in that graveyard since the First World War!"

Gott's eyes smouldered viciously. "Of course Mister expert bloody historian Williams would know that, wouldn't he? Probably got it from expert bloody historian brother of his – same one as did his last History essay for him, eh lads?"

"That's right, cheat!" Shorty spat.

"And now he's got the lovely Miss Grey to help him. Miss Lah-di-dah, bloody-posh-bitch Grey," Gott snarled.

"Show you to her bedroom, did she?" Shorty giggled.

Jamie's patience was wearing thin and his tormentors sensed it. "Thanks, Jamie . . . Thanks for your help!" Gott mimicked again. "What have you been helping her to do, you naughty little boy?" he leered.

Jamie's hand clenched the leather book tightly and he made a fist with the other. He could knock Gott over with one punch and probably turn on Shorty before the tall boy had a chance to move. But Podge wasn't drunk. He was standing, sulkily, silently behind the other two. He looked slow and stupid and fat. But Jamie knew he was more muscle than fat and what he lacked in brain he made up in vicious fighting tricks. He'd been caught at one football match for carrying a knife and Jamie knew that he still carried it when he thought he could get away with it.

He would lose a fight. He could outrun them, but he'd never be able to face them in school again. He'd just have to humour them. "Jealous, are you, Eric?" and he attempted a grin.

"Nah, she's not my type. I'm no snob," the thin boy replied.

"No, just a yob," Jamie said lightly. Then he

20

realised he'd made a mistake. Gott stepped back. Out of the reach of Jamie now.

"Trying to be funny, Williams?"

"No, I . . ."

"Well, if you're not trying to be funny you must be serious." He turned to his friends. "Hear that, lads? He's calling us yobs!"

Podge and Shorty took it as a cue to move forward. Jamie put his hands out defensively. Something in the gesture caught Gott's eye. "What have we here, lads?" he asked. He lunged forward and snatched the leather diary from Jamie's hand.

"What is it, Rick?" Shorty asked.

"Just some old book," Gott sneered. "Here, catch!" He flung the book towards the tall boy.

Jamie made a sudden move to intercept the throw and missed. The gang realised they had the makings of some sport. "Here! Can you read, Podge?" Shorty cried and threw it to his sullen mate.

"Give it back, Hodge," Jamie said.

"Or what?"

"Or he'll tell his mammy!" Gott jeered. "Chuck it here, Podge. Might be some of that 'original source material' old Waites was going on about."

The fat boy threw the book carelessly at his gang leader. A loose page flew out and fluttered to the ground while the diary hit the beer can in Gott's outstretched hand. Both can and book fell to the greasy pavement.

Gott scrambled to save his spilling beer, cursing at Hodge and Short and at anyone else he could think of. Jamie took the opportunity to swoop and collect the old book. He tucked it into the pocket of his anorak and walked quickly away into the foggy night, being careful not to run.

Gott drained what was left of his beer then threw the can angrily after him. "What a waste! What a crying, bloody waste. Here, Shorty, what you got there?" he asked.

"I've got one of those pages that fell out of the book," the tall boy said, moving closer to the lamp-post to catch the orange light.

"Throw it away," Gott ordered.

"Nah! Hang on, Rick. This is interesting. Very interesting. It's not a page from the book, it's a letter. And look what it says!"

"Give it here, then," the gang leader ordered. He shook his head to clear the beer fumes and studied it carefully. "Hell's teeth!" he breathed finally.

"What are we going to do, Rick?" Shorty asked.

"We need the help of an expert," Gott said carefully.

"Not Jamie Williams's brother?"

"Nah. Someone else." He looked up with a crooked grin. "We're going to go in for a bit of real historical research, lads. Old Mr Waites would be proud of us!" He folded the sheet of paper carefully, slipped it into his pocket and hurried off eagerly.

Jamie felt better after an hour at Robert's house. His brother had been enthusiastic about taking on the interpretation of the diary and insisted on working on it there and then. Pushing aside a pile of marking on his untidy desk, he pulled an angled lamp down to study the small neat writing, switched on the small computer and began entering a mass of complicated data.

Jamie phoned home to explain that he'd be staying at Robert's house that night, then settled down to watch some television while his brother worked.

Occasionally Robert's head would rise from the cloud of pipe smoke to announce some discovery. Jamie just nodded and smiled. He knew his brother was talking to himself as much as to him. "Not in code . . . more a sort of shorthand . . . mentions her sixteenth birthday here . . . dated 1831, that means she was born in 1815 – year of the battle of Waterloo, you know?"

Jamie just smiled. He knew. Ten years ago, when Robert had been his age and Jamie had been just six, the older brother used to swamp him with a mass of dates and facts. Day trips were never to the nearby coast but to museums and historical monuments. Jamie had learned a lot and impressed everyone with his knowledge. "You're just like your brother," family friends would say.

But that wasn't true. It was true the two *looked* alike with their sandy hair and light-brown eyes, but Robert's eyes lit up at the sight of an old book while Jamie's lit up at the sight of a football.

Jamie was dozing in the warmth of the flat when Robert stretched and rose from the table. He handed his younger brother a sheaf of computer printout paper and said, "That's a start, anyway. I'll take the rest to the university and work on it in my spare time."

"Thanks, Rob. Will it be of any use to us?"

"I think so. Not a lot of historical detail but a fascinating story. The diary belonged to a girl called Marie Grey, older daughter of Joshua Grey, the industrialist, and his wife Caroline."

"I know that," Jamie interrupted. "I've seen her portrait at Grey Manor. She's beautiful."

Rob went on, "Judging by the writing I'd say she'd been quite well educated – unusual even for a wealthy girl in those days. Fathers usually preferred their daughters to learn the skills of housekeeping and of making a good wife. The result is young Marie seems a bit more 'liberated' than some of her contemporaries – strong-willed, with a mind of her own. Must have been a bit of a handful for her father, I think. I could be wrong, but reading between the lines I think he rather spoiled her, and I think she knew how to twist him round her little finger." Jamie always admired the way his brother could make the people of the past come alive. That was his great skill as a historian. "Quite a character, your Marie. Pity she was middle-class."

"What do you mean?" Jamie asked.

Robert rubbed his stubble beard tiredly. "I mean that when she grew up she'd become a typical Victorian matron – narrow-minded and against any form of progress. She would also place more value on possessions than on people. In fact people would become like possessions – she would have servants and she'd treat them no better than slaves. No one has the right to take away another person's freedom."

Jamie felt a cold slug of disgust slither up his spine at the thought of the lively Marie growing old and stale. Old and dying. "You can't be sure, Rob – you can't!"

Rob looked at his worried brother and smiled. He rubbed his hair roughly. "No, kid, I can't be sure. But when I've finished this diary I'll find out more about this Marie Grey when she grew up – find out from the records who she married, what sort of household she ran. We'll see."

"Not Marie," Jamie said, reaching out and stroking the soft leather cover of the diary.

"If you can reach back into the past and feel for a girl who's been dead a hundred years – well, we'll make a historian of you yet. That's what History is really about. Not dates and bones and dust. People. People like you and me."

"And Trish?"

"Who's Trish?"

"Oh, just some middle-class girl I know. I think she's some sort of great-great grand-daughter of the diary girl, Marie Grey."

Rob put on a mock-fierce face. "Keep away from the middle classes, my boy! Before you know it they'll corrupt you with their greedy values. Have you owning your own house before you're twenty-five."

"Like you do, Rob?" Jamie asked wickedly.

His brother cuffed him playfully round the head and bundled him off to the spare room to sleep. "But I haven't read the diary yet!" Jamie objected.

"Plenty of time for that tomorrow. Save it as a treat to read with that middle-class girlfriend of yours."

"She's not my girlfriend!" Jamie objected a little too quickly.

Rob smiled. "No, but you fancy her. Goodnight! Sleep tight!"

But Jamie's sleep was troubled by dreams of ghosts and graves. Of a black-haired girl with a deep blue dress . . . and of treasure hoards.

Chapter Three

By the next evening the fog had given way to a steady drizzle. Jamie hurried, head down, along Manor Walk past the deserted graveyard. The heavy cloud was bringing an early evening to Seawell and the lights of the shipyards were dazzling on the river.

The boy slowed and pushed his wet hair from his forehead as he neared the entrance to the graveyard. Too wet for a beer party tonight, he thought. Yet he could have sworn that he saw some movement among the grey-green stones and shining marble slabs. Over in the centre of the graveyard was a small stone building – almost a one-roomed house, slate-roofed and with fine arched door and windows. The windows were bricked up but the door seemed to be blowing gently to and fro.

Jamie shook the rain from his hair and decided that was the movement he'd seen. He walked on to the huge iron gates at the entrance to Grey Manor – gates rusted open after years of disuse. In the half-light of evening it looked even sadder than in the foggy shadows of the night before. Weeds fought with flowers for space on the garden and spilled over on to the gravelled drive.

He stopped at the front door and tried to drag a comb through the tangle of his hair. He was half afraid of seeing Trish again, and even more afraid of seeing her father. "He practically threw me out last night!" he'd argued with Trish that day in school.

"He'd had a bad day at work," she'd said. "He'll be all right if you come round tonight, I promise."

"Can't I just give you the first transcript of the diaries now?" Jamie had moaned.

"No," Trish said firmly. "We have to go through them together."

"Break time, like we agreed."

Trish had turned away from him and pretended to arrange books in her bag. "The others in the class . . ." she began awkwardly. "The boys especially. No, that's not true . . . the girls as well. They're . . . you know, making comments about us."

"Comments?"

"Comments!" she'd said tersely. "You must have heard them!"

He'd shrugged. "Eric Gott said we must fancy one another, but . . ."

"Well, there you are then. I'm not having people

making insinuations like that about us just because we chose to work together. How dare they say I fancy you!"

"Why, what's wrong with me?" he'd cried.

She'd known she'd said the wrong thing. "I didn't mean it like . . . oh, Jamie, why can't you be reasonable and just come round to Grey Manor this evening?" And she'd left him sitting at his desk.

For the rest of the day she'd avoided his glances and ignored his presence in the room just as she had for the last five years. His closest friends, the ones he played football with, had sensed his misery and tried in their clumsy way to console him. "Ah man, Jamie. She's too classy for the likes of you."

"Thanks very much," he'd muttered.

And now he hesitated at the door again. Perhaps he could just push the computer printout through the letterbox and go home. As he reached out the door swung open.

"Ah, James! There you are! Do come in, my boy!"

If Jamie was shocked at seeing Mr Grey at the door he was completely dumbfounded by the warm greeting.

"I've come to see Trish," the boy said.

"Of course you have. Of course you have. To do with this History project at school, isn't it? Not like in my day," the man said as he led the way into the hall. "Let's go to the library. Trish has lit a fire – dry you out nicely. No, in my day we just learned facts from books and then we were tested to see if we'd remembered them. Let me take your coat – you're dripping on the carpet."

Jamie allowed himself to be led past the portrait of the blue-eyed girl and into the library. This evening, the fire almost filled the long grate. Even the bulb in the table lamp seemed brighter; it lit an assortment of papers and open books that were carefully arranged to cover the surface of the table.

"Trish . . .?" Jamie started to say.

"In the kitchen," her father explained. "Making us tea. Since her mother left my daughter has done all of the cooking – good training for when she finally marries." He shook his head sadly. "My only daughter, alas," he sighed.

"Why is that sad?" Jamie asked. "She's lovely . . . er . . . a very nice girl."

"Of course, of course. But you see, when I die Grey Manor will go to her. If she marries then she will no longer be a Grey. The Grey family – Grey with an 'e' not the more common Gray with an 'a' – the Grey family have lived at Grey Manor for centuries and I have traced my ancestors back to the times of Queen Elizabeth." The man pushed a book across the table. "That's the Grey coat of arms awarded to Sir Thomas Grey by Charles the First. He fought against Cromwell's roundheads, you know. All those years of tradition will die with me! No more Greys at Grey Manor."

"That's sad," Jamie said because he felt that's what he ought to say. Mr Grey's hard face looked warmer in the reflected blaze of the fire but Jamie still couldn't lose his fear of the man.

"It's more than sad. It's tragic. You're a historian, young man . . ."

"Well, I . . ."

". . . so you know how it was in the old days. So simple. The buildings were as fine as Grey Manor. Look at the slums we build now!"

"But the poor people in the old days lived in appalling . . ." Jamie tried to argue.

"Ah, yes, the poor people were so much happier in those days!" Mr Grey said vigorously.

Jamie remembered his brother's description of the miseries of the poor of Seawell. "Happier?"

"Ah, yes. You see, they knew their place. They would have been penniless if the rich hadn't created the labouring jobs and the serving jobs for the poor. Why, the rich even built houses for the poor so they would be near their jobs." Jamie opened his mouth but Mr Grey held up a hand and went on. "Oh, I know that what I'm saying isn't very fashionable among modern historians like your brother – a brilliant young man, by the way – but I think that time will prove me right. Let's get back to the good old days and see a return to true happiness for humanity. That's what I'm working for!"

"Working for? I thought you were a lawyer, Mr Grey."

"True, true. I meant what I'm working for in my spare time – my historical research into the past of Grey Manor and the Grey family," the man explained.

"How will that help to restore the past?" Jamie asked, confused.

Mr Grey leaned forward to speak confidentially. "There is a treasure belonging to the Grey family, and it is hidden somewhere quite close by. It was hidden by Joshua Grey before he died in 1835. Unfortunately the clues to its whereabouts have been lost over the years, but I am convinced that those clues lie in this library. When I find the treasure I will restore Grey Manor to its full glory. We will have servants to cook and to clean, servants to keep the gardens in good order and servants to wait upon us at our meals. In the meantime we'll have to make do with my dear daughter. Here she is now!"

Trish slipped into the room with a tray. Pushing aside one or two books she made room for tea cups and plates of cake. She greeted Jamie with a warm smile. "Pour tea, Trish," Mr Grey ordered. His daughter obeyed silently but it made Jamie feel uncomfortable to see her fitting into her father's plan for the world.

"Has Father been boring you with his stories about the Greys?" she asked as she passed a cup to him.

"It's fascinating," Jamie said, and in a strange way it did intrigue him to learn about Trish's background. "I was just wondering . . . how can you be so sure about the existence of this treasure?"

"Don't ask!" Trish said quickly.

But Jamie had asked, and Mr Grey went to great lengths to explain. It seemed it was his pet subject and he needed no second invitation to tell the story.

This evening he already had the "proofs" spread out on the table.

"The mystery surrounds Joshua Grey and something that happened between 1830 and 1835," he began with a well-rehearsed speech.

Jamie listened intently, for the diary of Marie was for the year 1831. It could all make good background knowledge for his project with Trish.

Joshua Grey was the owner of the Grey family lands in Durham County in the 1820s. A modestly wealthy family who earned their money by renting some land to tenant farmers and keeping sheep or cattle on other land of their own. Then, in 1823, coal was found under the Grey land and Joshua Grey decided to mine it.

"Of course a few peasant farmers were sent packing," Mr Grey explained, "but they were offered jobs down the new mines."

"That's not the same. Farmers don't want to be miners!" Trish objected.

"Strange to say they didn't. They chose to go to the poorhouse instead," her father said harshly. "Idle fools! Anyway, Joshua Grey mined the coal but had trouble getting it all the way to London to sell. That's when he had the brilliant idea that really made his fortune."

"Yes, Father," Trish nodded and explained, "It seemed that Joshua Grey had land on the banks of the River Wear. So he built docks on the Wear to load ships to carry the coal to London."

Mr Grey leaned forward eagerly. "And most

brilliant of all, he built one of the world's first railway systems to carry the coal from the mines to the docks. The complete system, and he owned it all! Mines, railways, docks. Of course he invited wealthy colleagues to share in the booming new town of Seawell – just a village before Joshua Grey came. The Fawcetts came and made shipyards to build the ships; the Macmillans came to build the ironworks that supplied the railways, the shipyards and the mines. The three great families had the town of Seawell sewn up between them. Look at the accounts of Grey's companies for 1829!" Mr Grey crooned and pushed a page of figures at Jamie.

The boy was bewildered by the scrawl of numbers. Mr Grey pointed to a figure at the bottom. "One hundred and seventeen thousand pounds profits that year from the sale of coal alone. That represents millions of pounds by today's values."

"But even if you found the hundred thousand pounds it's hardly enough to rebuild Grey Manor and fill it with servants," Jamie said.

Mr Grey looked smug. "Joshua was no fool. Look!" and he pushed a slip of paper across the table. This time Jamie was able to read it.

"Received from Joshua Grey the sum of one thousand guineas in full payment for one diamond necklace and matching earrings." He looked up. "Jewels?"

"Yes, my boy! Joshua turned the profits into jewels. When we find these jewels . . . and these . . . and these . . ." he said picking up a pile of similar receipts, "we will be richer than anyone in Seawell! That receipt you have for a thousand guineas must be for a necklace worth a hundred thousand today, and that's just one small item in this treasure."

"So what happened to it? Perhaps it was stolen. Perhaps business slumped and he lost his fortune," Jamie argued.

"Father has the business returns for every year till Joshua died in 1835, and every year they show a greater profit," Trish began.

"But no more receipts for jewels after 1831. Lots of money coming in – none going out," Mr Grey went on. "Then, at his death in 1835, we have his will. He leaves Grey Manor to his younger daughter, Louise. She has married a cousin, George Grey, so the Grey family name remains."

"What about Marie, the older daughter?" Jamie asked.

Mr Grey shrugged. "No mention. Perhaps she was deliberately cut out of the will. She was, by all accounts, a wilful, obstinate girl."

"And his wife?"

"Died just before him in 1835."

Jamie nodded. It did seem odd. "What did the will say about the fortune?" he asked suddenly.

Mr Grey smiled craftily. "Clever of you to think of that, my boy. There is just one mention. I'll read it. It says '*My Treasure is buried. By the time you read this I shall be buried too. I trust that my wealth may bring peace and happiness to others in the future, a happiness it never brought to me.*'"

Jamie thought through the words. "His wealth brought him unhappiness, so he buried it. Is that what you think it means?"

"What else could it mean?" Mr Grey asked eagerly.

"And the mention of bringing happiness to others?" Jamie asked.

"It would bring Father great happiness if he found it," Trish said wryly.

"That's it," Mr Grey agreed. "Peace and happiness."

"And all we have to do is find the treasure," Trish said.

"I wish you luck," Jamie said.

Mr Grey smiled at the boy. "You can do more than that. You can help."

"How?"

"Last night . . . I was a little upset . . . trouble at the office, you understand. I hope I wasn't too abrupt with you?"

"Oh, no!"

"What Father's trying to say is that after you left he started thinking about Marie, the older daughter who wrote the diary," Trish explained.

"Yes," Mr Grey went on. "You mentioned her omission from the will. A small matter but it could be important. It could be the last piece of the jigsaw that makes the rest make sense."

"I have the first part of my brother's transcription here!" Jamie offered eagerly.

But Mr Grey's smile slipped. "That may be useful,

but what I really want is the diary. If you'll just give it back to me I can give you lots of other material suitable for your project at school."

"But I don't have it," Jamie said.

"What?" Mr Grey said harshly. "Where is it?"

"My brother took it to the university to work on," Jamie explained.

Mr Grey rose to his feet. He was trembling. "I want that diary back and I want it now!"

Jamie rose too. "I'll bring it tomorrow."

"Tonight!"

"Father!" Trish cried. "It doesn't matter that much! Surely another night . . ."

"I don't want it in the hands of scum like that Robert Williams. He shan't have the secret of the Grey Treasure! He shan't! Tonight!" and he flung himself out of the room.

Trish was shaking. "Sorry, Jamie. Sorry. I've never seen him so angry before. I don't understand. Last night he threw it at you; tonight he wants it back. What's happened between then and now to change his mind?"

Jamie shook his head slowly. "I don't know. I don't know. Perhaps Rob would know."

"Would you mind calling tonight?" the girl asked as she began collecting the cups and plates in a distracted manner.

"Of course. I mean, no. Rob works late on Tuesdays. Sometimes he even stays at Durham if it gets too late. I could phone and find out," he offered.

"The only phone is in Father's room. I'd rather not disturb him . . ."

"That's OK. There's a callbox opposite the graveyard. I'll use that!"

He reached across and touched Trish lightly on the hand. She froze for a moment then looked up with a flicker of a smile. "Thanks, Jamie," she murmured.

He hurried out into the quiet night. The rain had stopped and the air smelled fresh after the staleness of Grey Manor. A half moon was gliding out of the clouds and glimmering on the wet cobbles of Manor Walk, and by its light Jamie could see that the phonebox was occupied. Three youths. A small one, a tall thin one and a square, heavy one. He slid into the shadow of Grey Manor gates and waited. A minute later Eric Gott stepped out with his two friends. A light wind carried snatches of their words to Jamie's ears: " . . . doesn't get it tomorrow . . . steal it . . . ten quid *each*!" And then they were gone.

Jamie ran to the phone and called Rob's home. There was no reply. Five minutes later he'd found the number of the university and reached his brother.

"Sorry, kid – tell the old goat he'll have to wait. I've done a second part of the diary and it's getting interesting. I knew I wouldn't be home tonight so I posted it to you. You should have it in the morning post. See you tomorrow night! Bye."

Jamie cursed softly. He walked back to pass on the

bad news to Trish. "Never mind," she said. "I'll tell him later."

Jamie felt guilty about leaving the unpleasant task to Trish, and secretly glad when she insisted that it would be easier for her.

"I'll see you tomorrow at school. We have to make a first presentation of our researches to the class," he reminded her.

Her velvet-blue eyes widened. "We can't. We haven't been through it together."

"Have you time now?" Jamie asked.

"Of course," Trish said eagerly. "It's hours before bedtime and I don't have any other homework. Do you?"

"Oh, no!" Jamie lied. "I'd just be at home watching television."

"Sometimes I wish we had one," she said wistfully. "Father says that we can't afford it."

"There's not that much on worth watching," he said, trying to console her.

"Probably not, it's just that the other girls like to talk about the programmes they've watched the night before."

"And you feel left out?"

Trish nodded. "They think I stay out of the conversations because I'm . . . . a snob!"

"Oh, I'm sure they don't think that!" Jamie said.

The girl looked at him from under her level eyebrows. "Come on, Jamie. I bet you've said it yourself."

"No, I . . ." he began to protest. He felt a blush rising to his face. "I used to. I'm sorry."

"That's all right," Trish said seriously. "It's nothing to what I used to say about you!"

Jamie winced. "And now?"

"And now I think *I* may have been wrong. And you?" she admitted.

"And now I think I may have been wrong."

"So let's look at my Great-great-great-great Aunt Marie's diary," she suggested.

They bent their heads over the library table and read.

Chapter Four

Jamie,

Here is Marie Grey's notebook. It's not really a diary, just a place where she sometimes jotted down her thoughts and experiences. I've skipped some of the boring detail and added notes where I think you might need them. Otherwise it's the authentic words of Marie Grey, born with a silver spoon in her mouth in 1815, died I don't know when – but I'll find out.

Cheers,
Rob

I hate my mother. Boring old besom – that's a word I've heard Molly use and I think it's pretty rude!

Molly was her personal maid. I'm afraid "besom"

was just a local word for "floor-brush"! Sorry, I'll try not to interrupt too much – Rob.

The boring old besom has given me this book, quills and ink-pot and told me to practise my handwriting. 'A lady should be skilled and neat in writing. When she presents the monthly housekeeping accounts to her husband they should be a work of art! Besides, your father paid a fortune to send you to that good school, so let us see you writing!'

But it's summer. From my room I can see the sea. I want to go there and watch the bathers on the beach. I want to walk along the promenade in my deep blue cotton dress with its matching parasol. Everyone would look at me. Molly says the dress matches my eyes and that I look beautiful. But what is the use of looking beautiful if there is no one to see my beauty? And how will I find myself a husband if I'm not allowed out in public – except to go to church – and then I wear that huge and ugly bonnet.

I suppose the answer is that I won't find myself a husband. I suppose my parents will find him for me. I know my father will choose well. He has taste. He is the best dressed man in Seawell, probably in the whole county of Durham. But if the boring old besom has anything to do with it she'll choose the most boring and ugly man she can find. She has already dropped the name of Horatio Macmillan in my pretty ears.

[Horatio was oldest son of the ship-building Macmillan family, born 1805 in the year of the battle of Trafalgar – Rob]

Horatio Macmillan! Horrors! He doesn't hunt or shoot or gamble or wear fine clothes. He wears sight-

correctors for his squint and he's half a foot shorter than me. I sometimes wonder what he spends his share of the family fortune on. I suppose, if he married me, then he could spend the fortune on me! But to be seen in public with such a man! How can one dance with a man who's a full foot shorter than one? Emma would laugh – she's such a snob.

[Probably Emma Fawcett, eldest daughter of the iron-works Fawcett family, born 1814 – Rob]

Emma plans to marry my cousin George. He's no better. He's only twenty and he's so fat he already wears a corset stronger than father's! Anyway, Lou also wants to marry George! They can fight over him. They can each have half – there's plenty of him!

[Lou will be Marie Grey's sister, Louise, born 1816, hence a year younger than Marie. Three years after this diary was written I believe that Louise did in fact marry her cousin George – Rob]

Seawell men are so short and fat and boring! I wish sometimes I lived in London. Perhaps I'll run away on one of Father's ships.

I can see the river crowded with them now. I'd cut my hair and dress up like a boy – they do it all the time in Shakespeare's plays and Scott's novels! I'd learn to swear like all the sailors. I'd eat hard ships' biscuits even if they were full of maggots as they say. I'd never wash and I'd fall in love with the ship's most handsome officer. We'd sail to some small island in the South Seas and live like Crusoe and Woman Friday! I'd paddle in the sea just as I used to when Lou and I were children.

I want to do that now! No, not to the South Seas. Just

to walk along Seawell promenade. It's summer. I'm tired with all this writing. I'm going to find myself adventure – The Old Besom will never find out. And if she does, and if she's angry, I'll throw myself on Father's mercy. He could never be hard on his darling Marie. I'd smile at him and say, "I'm sorry, Papa. Forgive me?"

And he would say, "Of course, you wicked girl! Just don't let your mother catch you again!"

And Lou will be furious because she's Mama's pet, but Mama is harder on her than my sweet Father is on me!

But enough of writing practice. I am decided. I'm going out for an adventure.

Jamie sat back in the library chair and rubbed his eyes. Trish looked at him. "Well?" she said.

"Well . . . Rob was right," Jamie said. "Seems to be a real little madam, spoilt by her father. Notice the way that even in her fantasy it's a ship's *officer* she plans to run away with, not some common sailor."

"I like her," Trish said simply.

Jamie smiled. "I liked her as soon as I saw her portrait. Now I'm not so sure. Seems a bit of a snob."

"But half an hour ago you admitted that you thought *I* was a snob!" Trish pointed out.

"That's different," Jamie muttered unhappily. He didn't want to argue with Trish, but he didn't want to back down either.

"Look," Trish persisted. "You were right. I *was* a snob. I didn't like to speak to you or your friends. I was . . . but only because I'm shy. So I didn't want to mix with people I didn't know. And because I didn't know you I was a little afraid of you. If that's being a snob then I was a snob."

"But you're changing," Jamie said.

"Only because I'm coming to know you, know that there's nothing to be afraid of," she explained. "Don't you try to avoid people you're afraid of?"

"No . . ." he began. And he remembered seeing the Gott gang in the phonebox earlier that night. And he remembered hiding in Grey Manor gateway until they'd gone. "Yes," he said quietly. "But Marie Grey is – or *was* – so self-centred. She's only interested in herself!"

"That's because she was encouraged to think of herself. If you had a servant who told you how beautiful you were, a father who adored you, friends who competed with you to attract the best of a few eligible men, then *you'd* be self-centred. But she could change."

Jamie sighed. "I hope so. I'd like the girl in the portrait to turn out as good as she looks."

Trish gave him an odd look.

"Give her a chance," she urged. "Even if we don't find a Marie Grey that you like we still have to go on looking for a clue to the treasure!"

That was true, Jamie reflected. He turned to the next sheet of notes.

[There are no dates on this notebook. The following

45

seems to have been written some time after the previous passage, perhaps the next day – Rob]

I have had my adventure. I have to write it here because I would not dare to tell Emma my thoughts. They are too shocking to be shared with even my best friend. Perhaps this book will prove to be a better friend after all.

Mother was at a church council meeting. I called Molly and told her to prepare my blue cotton dress.

"Are you going out, Miss?" she asked.

"It's not your business to enquire where I'm going. It's your business to do as you're told," I said sharply.

Molly is a sweet and helpful child but not blessed with too many brains. I hate to speak to her sharply but Mama says that's the way we must always speak to servants. "Servants like it," she says, "because then they are content to know their place." But, after my adventure, now I'm not so sure. The Old Besom knows a lot, I'll give her that, but perhaps she doesn't know everything.

I put on my finest silk stockings and blue buckled shoes, my newest undergarments and lastly my blue cotton dress. Cotton from India. Still quite rare in Seawell. "Fetch me a bowl of water and a sponge, Molly," I said.

"A bowl of water and a sponge?" she repeated stupidly.

I sighed. I'd spoken to her sharply once and didn't want to again. I think I just pulled my eyebrows together and made my lips tight and impatient. She scurried off and came back minutes later with the bowl and sponge. She looked so worried I had to have some fun.

"What's wrong, Molly?" I asked as I took the bowl and placed it on the table.

"Well, Miss, it's just that you washed yourself this morning before you dressed. It's not like you to wash twice in one day, Miss."

"I don't want the water for washing in, Molly," I said.

I placed the wet sponge on my throat and drew it over my bosom and down to my waist. Molly's face was a picture. "Oh, Miss! You've wet your lovely dress!" she groaned.

I repeated the sponging until the top was soaked then passed the sponge to Molly. "Wet my back!" I ordered.

Still moaning and muttering and shaking her head, she obeyed. I really wished that Emma had been there to see it. We had talked about doing this for hours, wondering if either would dare to ever do it, and now I had!

Molly was gaping and letting the sponge dribble on to my best Persian rug. "I suppose you're wondering why I did that, Molly?"

"No, Miss. You was washing the dress, Miss!" she said.

I gave a small sigh then explained. "The damp of the dress makes it cling to my body, Molly."

"Yes, Miss."

"And so it shows off every curve of my body," I told her.

Her eyes were wide as saucers. "Ohh! Isn't that sinful, Miss? What would Mrs Grey say?"

"It is not sinful, Molly. Women in London have been doing it for years. And as for my mother she will not say anything because she will not know anything about it . . . and you will not tell her."

"No, Miss."

"Now tell Ellis to bring the chaise carriage to the front door in five minutes."

"We're going out, Miss?"

"We are going to the seaside, Molly."

And I knew how it felt to be mistress of a house for an afternoon. It was wonderful to have the house at my command – and frightening! If Mother should find out then not even Father would be able to save me!

But things did not go quite as I'd planned. When we reached the bridge over the Wear we were stopped at the toll gate.

There was a boy there, arguing with the toll man. "You have to let me across," he was pleading. "If I'm late for work I'll get the sack!"

Molly went stiff at my side. "My young brother, John!"

"It's a penny to cross, you know that, young Brown!" the old toll man said flatly.

"I've left my money at home. Let me across and I'll pay you double tomorrow!" the boy pleaded.

The toll man gave a harsh laugh. "If you knew how many times I've heard that story! And If I believed one I'd have to believe them all. If you have a penny at home then go and get it . . ."

"I'm late enough already!"

48

"And if you only have a halfpenny then take the ferry."

"That takes forever!" the boy cried and tried to push past the toll gate keeper. But the old man was ready for him. He had a heavy ash-plant stick and he jabbed it into the boy's stomach. The poor boy fell to the ground in pain. Molly gave a small sob. I suppose her brother was no older than I but so thin it seemed that there was no flesh between his skeleton and his skin.

"Leave him alone!" I cried.

The toll man looked up at me in my chaise and smiled. "Afternoon, Miss Grey. Fine afternoon for a drive," he said and raised his grubby blue cap.

"Why did you do that to the boy?" I asked.

"He's just one of the Brown family. Biggest load of lying villains in Seawell!"

"That's not true," Molly said, torn between her duty to stay with me and her desire to help her brother.

"I'll pay to let him cross the bridge," I offered.

"Thank you, Miss," Molly murmured.

The old man shrugged. "That's a penny for the boy and threepence for your carriage, Miss Grey."

"Pay the man fourpence, Ellis," I said. The coachman turned and shook his head.

"Sorry, Miss. Only Mr Grey has that sort of money."

"Molly?"

"You didn't ask me to bring your purse, Miss," she said.

The toll man smiled and showed his rotting black teeth. "All right, Miss, you go ahead. Mr Grey can pay next time he crosses."

49

"I didn't want my father to know I was out!" I snapped.

He gave me an ugly wink. "I understand. You go ahead and we'll say no more about it. Perhaps you can do me a favour some time!"

"Drive on, Ellis!" I said quickly before I made some hasty reply to his awful suggestion. I didn't like the way he was looking at my damp dress that was steaming now in the sun. I felt more foolish, angry and ashamed than I'd ever done in my life.

"But the boy stays here," the toll man leered.

Young Brown was on his knees now, watching the argument. "Get in the coach, Brown!" I ordered. I was defying the toll man to stop us now.

The boy scrambled into the carriage and gave a quick grin to his sister. He touched the peak of his cap to me. "Thanks, Miss." He half crouched on the cream leather seat opposite. His filthy clothes would mark the leather, and I'd be in trouble with Father. Then the toll man called after us. "So I'll be asking your father for four pence tonight when he comes home!" he cried and spat vulgarly after the carriage.

There was only one thing to do. Brazen it out with Father. "Take me to Mr Grey's office at the North Dock, Ellis!" I said.

Molly gasped and even Ellis looked worried, but he turned the ponies towards the dockside path.

Young John Brown sat silent and tugged at the holes in his trousers to cover his thin, pale legs. Molly stared fixedly at the chaise floor and avoided the curious stares of the sailors and dockers as we passed along the quayside. But I looked out. I had nothing to be ashamed of except, perhaps, my dress. Indeed, I had much to be proud of. Of every two ships at that harbour one flew the flag of the Grey family.

As we reached the ship named S.S. Grey Pride, young Brown looked up for the first time. He had wide brown eyes like his sister, but those eyes held no fear or respect for me. Indeed they seemed full of life and fun. I wondered how he could live in such misery and have eyes so full of happiness. "If you'd let me off here, Miss, I'll get to work on that boat!"

"You work for my father?" I asked, surprised.

"Not for much longer if I don't get to work!" he grinned a cheeky grin.

"Don't let me keep you, Brown," I said.

"Thanks, Miss," he said. And I was confused when he added to the grin a huge wink. I tried very hard to look shocked!

As he headed for the gangplank of S.S. Grey Pride the door of the customs office flew open and my father appeared.

"Brown!" he commanded. "Get in here at once. I want a word with you."

The boy's thin shoulders slumped in despair. He trudged towards the office. I'd never seen my father at work before. He seemed so different from the relaxed, indulgent man I knew at home.

Then he looked up and saw me. His stern face softened. "Marie!" he cried. "What on earth are you doing here?"

"Come to make sure you're working hard to make me

more money for dresses," I teased. Then I remembered the dampness of the one I was wearing and clutched my parasol in front of me.

He frowned a little. "You shouldn't really be down here alone, my treasure," he said.

I gave him my sweetest smile. "Not alone, Papa. I have Molly here and Ellis of course. And I am sixteen, you know."

He stroked his long moustache thoughtfully. "I suppose so, I suppose so. It's hard for a father to accept that his little girl is growing into a fine young lady. Wait a few minutes. I'll deal with this boy then perhaps we can drive around the dock together. I'll show you the Grey empire that will one day belong to your future husband."

I stepped from the carriage and signalled Molly to wait there. I strolled alongside Father on his way to the office. "Papa, will you do something for me?"

"Anything, my chuck. You know you only have to ask."

"Papa, that boy – Brown. Don't dismiss him," I said.

My father stopped and looked at me sharply. "Why not? He deserves it!"

"Please, Papa?"

He gave agitated tugs at his moustache. "This is not the first time he has been late. It is the third time in September alone. No, no, no! He must be made an example of!"

"He is Molly's brother," I explained gently and rested my hand affectionately on his arm.

"Who's Molly?" he asked.

"My maid," I reminded him.

"Ah. Her. Of course."

"It would upset her terribly," I went on. "Give him one more chance. Just one. He won't be late again."

"I wouldn't bet on it," Father snorted.

"I would," I said carefully.

"Would what?"

"Bet on it," I said. And I know that my father's great weakness is gambling – horses, cock-fights, card games, dog-fights, anything!

"How much?" he asked.

"I'll wager my month's clothes allowance – ten guineas – that Brown isn't late again before Christmas," I offered.

Father smiled. "You'll lose. You don't know Brown!" he warned.

"I'll tell Molly to make sure I win. Is it a bet?"

"It's a bet," he agreed with a grin. He strode into his office while I hurried back to the chaise to break the news to Molly.

Two minutes later John Brown stumbled out of the office and blinked in the September sunlight, more dazed than pleased at his good fortune. Molly hurried to explain what had happened. He came to my chaise.

"Molly told me, Miss Grey. Thank you, Miss," he said and touched his cap.

"I have a lot of money and a lot of pride resting on you . . . John. Don't let me down."

And he grinned that cheeky grin again across his hungry, dirty face. "Don't worry, Miss. I won't let you

down. I promise, Miss!'' and he hurried off to help
unload the ship.

Somehow that smile meant more to me than any
money could. It was good to be mistress of Grey Manor
for the afternoon, to order servants and parade my
shameless self along the streets. But helping that poor,
poor boy meant more to me than anything.

Yesterday, like The Old Besom, I thought I knew
everything about life and people.

Now I feel I know nothing. Nothing.

Chapter Five

Jamie folded the papers carefully, thoughtfully. "No one has the right to take away another person's freedom," he said.

"What was that?" Trish asked. She'd made a fresh pot of tea and cupped her mug in her hands as she looked into the dying embers of the fire.

"Something my brother said last night," Jamie explained. "He said no one has the right to take away another person's freedom. He has this thing about servants and masters – thinks it's all wrong."

"Isn't it?" Trish asked.

Jamie was worried. "Yes, but Marie's notebook shows something else. It shows that she has no more freedom than John or Molly Brown. No freedom to go out where she wants, to marry whom she wants, or not marry if she wants. The Grey treasure would be no good to her anyway – her father said it would belong to her future husband. Maybe that's where it went. Maybe she married and her husband took it away."

"No," Trish argued. "The money was still coming in till the time of Joshua Grey's death. What was he spending it on? Remember, there's no mention of Marie in the will."

"I wonder why not. She was definitely his favourite daughter."

"Perhaps she married someone unsuitable, left home and he cut her from his will," Trish suggested.

"That's what must have happened, but what was Joshua spending his fortune on after she went?" Jamie wondered.

"I think I know the answer to that one," the girl said and poked at the last log till sparks crackled it back into life. "He was a gambler. He gambled on anything, remember? He must have lost his fortune that way."

Jamie rose from the library table and stretched. "That's it, then? No treasure and no mystery? Marie ran off with an unsuitable man and Joshua gambled away the treasure. Disappointed?"

"No," Trish said. "But Father would be. He'd never believe that. In fact something has happened to make him believe in the treasure more strongly than ever. I wonder what."

Jamie shrugged and picked up his coat. It was still damp from the earlier rain. He put it on slowly, reluctant to leave. "I should have part two of Marie's notes tomorrow," he said.

"And don't forget to return the notebook to father tomorrow night," she reminded him.

Jamie brightened. "I'll have to see you again then?"

"Of course. I'll see you in school."

"No. I meant . . . alone. Like this."

Trish's dark blue eyes studied him seriously. "We still have the rest of the notes to look at."

"And after the project's finished?"

"After?"

"We'll go back to ignoring each other in school."

"If that's what you want," she said.

"No!" he said quickly. "No, I didn't mean that."

She rose and faced him. Her deep eyes were level with his. She was close enough for him to smell her perfume. "Then what did you mean?"

He closed his eyes to concentrate. He had to get the words right. He might never have another chance. "When the project is over, when we have no need to meet, we could still go on meeting. We could go out together. We get on well." He opened his eyes to meet her steady gaze.

"It isn't that easy," she said.

"If you're worried about what the class will say then we'll keep it from them – only meet outside school."

She shook her head slowly. The glossy black hair shone in the light of the table lamp. "No. The problem is my father. You don't understand. I come

57

home from school and I have to cook and clean for him. If I do have any free time then he'd want to know where I was going and who I was going with."

"Surely he doesn't hate me that much!" Jamie gasped.

"He does," she said simply. As the boy opened his mouth to protest she went on quickly, "Not for your sake – for your brother's. Your brother stands for everything Father hates. You know that. Father will never accept you. He will tolerate you if he thinks you can help to find his treasure, but he'll never accept you."

"You don't have to do what your father wants," Jamie argued angrily.

"I do," she said, calm and still. "Mother grew tired of his obsession with the Grey family and its lost treasure. She went off with another man. That put her in the wrong in the eyes of the law. When the divorce was settled I was placed in his care legally. Until I'm eighteen."

"I'll wait till you're eighteen," the boy said wildly.

"He still wouldn't approve. He wants me to marry someone who will preserve the traditions of the Grey family. You'd never fit his requirements."

"You could leave him when you're eighteen!"

For the first time Trish's face hardened. "No I couldn't. He's my father. I'm all he's got!"

And Jamie lost his temper. "You're not his daughter – you're his slave! Rob's right – no one has the right to take away another person's freedom."

Two spots of colour began to glow in Trish's pale

cheeks and her eyes sparked anger too. "I have my freedom. It's what I choose to do."

"Sacrifice your life to look after him? Or marry a person of his choice not your own?" he cried. "I'll bet Marie wouldn't do that."

"What's Marie got to do with it?" she asked, bewildered.

"Marie had guts. I bet she broke out of the Grey stranglehold," he said.

"You don't know that," Trish argued.

"I can guess," he said sullenly.

"That's just what you want to believe. Do you know what I think?"

"I don't care."

"I think you're in love with her."

It was Jamie's turn to be bewildered. "In love with Marie? She's dead!"

"Not when you read her notebook she's not," the girl suggested. "Not when you're looking at her portrait. She's more alive than me!"

"I do admire her . . ."

"Love her!"

"And I bet she had the strength to go out with who she wanted. No matter how unsuitable he was. No matter how much her father disapproved," he argued.

"What? You imagine she'd dare to love someone like John Brown."

Jamie shook his head, confused. "John Brown? Who says she loved John Brown?"

"It's obvious to anyone with half a brain that she fell in love with John Brown the moment she saw him. Don't just read the words – read the feeling between the lines."

"This is so crazy," Jamie said, running a hand through his wild sandy hair. "But if she *did* love John Brown she'd go off with him. She'd have no reason to stay in that Grey Manor . . . I mean, this Grey Manor." He shivered at the sudden thought that Marie had once stood where he was standing now. Her ghost appearing now could not have disturbed him more.

"She had one good reason to stay here – the same as I have," she said fiercely. "It's something called duty. Something you and your brother wouldn't understand," she added spitefully.

"I understand," he flared. "I understand that it's not just your father who's against us – against us because we're not good enough to mix with the Godalmighty Greys. You even believe it yourself."

"And if I do?"

"And if you do then you really are the snob they say!" he finished, matching spite for spite.

He turned and walked out of the library. He felt the eyes of Marie's portrait following him down the hallway. He couldn't turn to meet her gaze. He fled and didn't stop running till he reached the graveyard.

He gripped the railings and sobbed for breath. He was shaking with emotion. Furious at the stupid, stupid way he'd handled things.

For fully five minutes he clung there, cursing, going over and over the argument and wondering where he'd gone wrong. But his breathing eventually slowed and the chill night air cooled him.

The sky was clear for the first time in days. The half moon lit the graveyard in crisp silver and black tones. Slowly his eyes began to see the derelict place clearly for the first time.

That strange little house in the centre, its door firmly closed against the night . . . firmly closed. But it had been open earlier that evening. Perhaps it had blown shut and jammed that way.

He looked at his watch. Still just half-past nine. He wasn't expected home till ten. Curiosity overcame his fear. He walked through the open gates and along the gravel path. For some reason he found himself walking on tiptoe as if his footsteps would waken the sleepers beneath the stones. No, he thought. He was more worried about the living, waking beings who might be in the stone house.

But the house was silent as any grave. The door was old with a heavy bolt on the outside and a padlock to keep out unwanted visitors. If the door was locked on the outside then there was no one inside, he reasoned. But that door had been open earlier this evening. So while he'd been with Trish someone had been prowling round the graveyard.

As Jamie turned and walked slowly back to the warmer glow of the lamps in the street a fine gravestone caught his eye. Not only was it larger than the other stones, but richer – a fine marble – and cleaner too. The only grave still tended by the look of it.

By the moon's dim light he made out the words.

Here Lies Joshua Grey
Born 1789 – Died 1835
also
his beloved wife
Caroline Grey
Born 1791 – Died 1835
also
. . . . .

But Jamie didn't want to see the alsos. There was one name he never wanted to see. *Marie Grey : born 1815 – died . . .*

He didn't want to know. The lively girl who had written those notes in his pocket wasn't dead. She couldn't be. She mustn't be. His brother's words were cruel enough! "She probably grew up to be some Victorian matron." But the thought of her dead and turned to dust under that tomb was unbearable.

He walked quickly along the path and back to the empty street. He crossed it, went into the phonebox and paused, resting his head against the cool perspex. Looking down and over the river he could see welding torches arc across the night, blue-white as lightning and caught himself trying to picture Marie in her carriage down among the wooden boats. Jamie sighed.

"All right, Trish," he muttered. "You're right and I was wrong. I let myself fall for an imaginary girl called Marie – your great-great-great-great aunt. I'm sorry, Trish. Lots of people fall in love with dreams – pop stars, film stars, sports stars that they never meet. I just didn't believe that it could happen to me."

He lifted the receiver, dropped in a coin and dialled her number.

It was answered almost immediately. "Edward Grey here."

"Could I speak to Trish, please?"

"Who's that calling?"

"Jamie Williams."

"Ah, young Williams. Do you have that diary for me yet?"

"No. Sorry. Trish said she'd explain – I suppose she's had no chance yet. My brother's staying the night at Durham University. He's hoping he'll be back tomorrow evening." Jamie held his breath during the silence that followed.

"I suppose that will have to do," Mr Grey said finally. "Goodnight!"

"Oh, Mr Grey!"

"Yes? What is it now?"

"Trish. Would it be convenient to speak to Trish?"

"Oh, very well . . . I'll get her now."

Jamie listened to the fading echo of footsteps at the other end of the phone, then he realised that he didn't know what he'd say to Trish when she answered.

"Hello? Jamie?"

"Hello, Trish."

"Yes?"

"I just wanted to say sorry, Trish . . . I said a lot of stupid things."

There was a long silence.

"So did I, Jamie."

"What?"

"I'm sorry too," she said quietly. He realised that it could be difficult for her talking if her father was in the room with her.

"Shall I still call tomorrow . . . with the second part of my brother's notes?"

"Yes . . . please."

"See you then."

"Yes."

"Goodnight."

"Goodnight."

"Goodnight!"

"Goodnight!"

The next morning Jamie collected his brother's letter with the second batch of notes and hurried to school without opening them.

Trish managed a quick, shy smile before the Humanities lesson – not much encouragement to show him their quarrel was forgotten, but better than nothing.

The presentation of their History investigations had to be done orally in front of the class. A slow business and after an hour of the lesson Jamie and Trish's turn hadn't come around.

"I look forward to hearing yours next week, Jamie and Trish," Mr Waites said. "Yours too, Eric Gott and Christopher Short. What is your choice of subject, by the way?"

Gott and Shorty exchanged a sly glance. "We'd rather not say, sir," the greasy-haired boy smirked. "Sort of special surprise."

"In other words you have no idea what you're going to do because you haven't lifted a finger since last lesson, have you, Eric?"

Gott was used to being accused of this sort of thing – and the accusations were usually true – but this time he looked genuinely upset by the teacher's suspicion. "We have, sir! We've been out every night working on it, haven't we, Shorty?"

"Yeah!" his lanky friend agreed. "Every night!"

"Perhaps you have something on paper you could show me?" Mr Waites asked mildly.

Gott clutched a manila folder to his chest. "It's secret, sir!"

Mr Waites nodded. "In that case you'd better come back for half an hour after school, Eric and Christopher. No one will be here to steal your secret."

"Aw, no sir!" the boy squawked and rose to his feet. "We've got more important work to do at four o'clock!"

"Important work, eh, Eric?" Mr Waites said, barely able to smother his smile.

"Yeah. Look, sir. If we show you what we've got so far will you let us off?"

"If what you have in that file is proof that you've seriously attempted a project then you are certainly free to pursue it further," the teacher agreed.

Reluctantly the boy passed the folder to the teacher, "Keep it secret, mind, sir!" he hissed.

Mr Waites took the folder back to his desk and shifted through the contents. His eyebrows rose till they almost disappeared into his grey fringe. "I am impressed, Eric. An . . . unusual subject . . . but fascinating. Interesting that Jamie and Trish are covering a related subject. Perhaps you should share your knowledge, eh?"

Gott's eyes slid across to Jamie. His expression was cunning and calculating. "Yeah, sir. Sounds like a good idea. I'll see him at break."

A bell rang and the classroom was half empty before the teacher called 'Class dismissed!'

Gott hung back. He nodded for Jamie to do the same but let Shorty and Trish leave. "What you got then, Williams?"

"A diary," Jamie said cautiously.

"Sounds interesting. Give us a look."

"My brother has it at the moment," Jamie said. "Sorry. He won't be home till after six tonight."

"Is that Robert Williams? Lives round the corner to us?"

"You know it is – he caught you nicking the wheel trims off his car one night last year," Jamie reminded him.

Gott's face turned fierce. "Yeah. Snitched to me parents for that. I got a belt," he snarled.

"It was either that or the police. You know what'll happen if the police have to deal with you again . . ."

"Yeah. OK, just get me that diary quick as you like, eh, Williams?"

The gang leader made to leave the room. Jamie stopped him. "Tell me, Eric, has this history project anything to do with the Manor Walk graveyard?"

The other boy's face reddened. "Mind your own pigging . . . well . . ." he collected himself. "It might do. It just might do. You get me that diary and I'll tell you what I'm working on. Deal?"

"I can't promise," Jamie began.

"What? Mr Waites says you've *got* to share! Teacher's pet like you wouldn't want to go against Mr Waites's instructions, would you?" he sneered.

Jamie kept his temper. "The diary is a historical artefact – probably very valuable – and it doesn't belong to me. I'll pick it up from my brother's flat this evening to return it to the owner."

"Lay off, Williams. We all know it belongs to your snobbish little blue-eyed girlfriend. With her 'Thank-you, Jamie . . . thanks for your help.' Well, you just tell her from me she'll give me a squint of that diary or get her lovely legs broke."

"Don't make threats you can't keep, Gott!" Jamie said and he felt his fists clench in his pocket. He didn't expect the boy to pick a fight when he didn't have his friends to back him, nor did he expect a complete climbdown.

But Eric Gott raised his hands in the air and smiled. "Sorry, Jamie, sorry! You know I'd never lay a finger on a young lady. Forget I said that. Let's just work together on this and help each other, eh?

After all, that's what friends are for."

He sauntered to the door, whistling.

Jamie was worried. Eric Gott as an enemy was a nuisance, but Eric Gott as a friend was deadly.

Trish was waiting for him by the classroom door. "Jamie, I've been thinking. Come round early tonight, say half-four, before Father gets back from work."

"OK," Jamie nodded. "Oh, but I won't have the original diary till Rob gets back at six."

"Never mind, you can collect it later." She went on quickly, trying to cover an awkwardness, "It's just that Father's trying to discourage me from working with you on this. It would be better if you came round when he wasn't there."

Chapter Six

That afternoon was the first time that Jamie had been in Grey Manor in daylight. He avoided looking at the portrait of Marie as Trish led him to the library again. The pale afternoon sun made the room look more dusty and worn than he remembered it.

They sat in the bay of the window that looked out over the deserted graveyard.

She said nothing about their quarrel. He didn't bring up the suggestion of their going out together. They were almost as distant as that first evening when she'd given him the diary.

It was depressing. He had to shake himself to take an interest in the papers in front of him. But soon he found himself engrossed in the world of Marie Grey.

[These notes seem to have been written quite a while after the last ones I gave you. Marie's shorthand seems more complex now, as if she's not just trying to write quickly, but trying to write secretly. Anyone picking up the 'diary' casually wouldn't understand it. But when you read it, I think you'll understand there were certain things she wanted no one to know – Rob.]

Since visiting Father's office and meeting John Brown a lot has happened. I've had little time to keep this notebook up to date. Now I'm in bed with a chill and time is dragging so I'll continue.

I've found out lots about the Brown family from Molly. I can't believe that they live in such dreadful squalor! Her father never works unless he has to, and when he does make money he spends it on cheap gin. She can't remember the last time she saw him sober. Her mother takes in washing just to make some money for the awful food they eat. Last night they made do with soup made from potatoes . . . skins and all!

John works hard but my father pays him very little. "Why not?" I asked Papa one day.

He laughed and said young ladies shouldn't try to understand men's business. "If we paid all our workers well they'd grow too fat and lazy. Our profits would go down and down until we all went bankrupt. Then we'd be poor and the men would be out of work. Ah, no! It makes no sense to pay the men a penny more than what they need to stay alive!"

"And if they grow too old or sick to work?" I asked.

"Then they go to the poorhouse. That's why I pay my

rates," he laughed. "To keep the borough poorhouse going and keep the beggars off the streets."

Mama, The Old Besom – she's no better. The wage she pays my Molly is a tenth of what I get for dress allowance every month!

"We feed the servants here," The Old Besom said, "much better than the fare they'd get at home. The maids work only sixteen hours a day and have a half-day off on Sunday. Just ask your Molly what she thinks. She'll tell you the servants have a happy life. They're proud to serve a family like the Greys!"

And Molly says that's true! Well, I'd not be a serving maid in anybody's house. I thought her home life must be truly dreadful if her work here in Grey Manor seems that much better. I decided, for my next adventure, that I'd visit Molly's home.

"You can't go there, Miss!" Molly gasped when I told her my plan.

"And what's to stop me going freely anywhere I want in Seawell?" I demanded.

She shook her head, "Oh, Miss, if some fine lady like yourself appeared in Low Street . . . I daren't think what they might do!"

"What who might do?"

"The ones from off the ships are worst! They'll rob you for the buckles on your shoes then sail off on the next high tide!" she whispered.

"Suppose I dressed in some disguise to make myself look poor?" I said.

She chewed her thumb and said, "Oh, Miss, there's more than thieves can do you harm in Low Street.

71

There's some disease they reckon brought in by the ships. You're not that strong, Miss. I remember how you were that sick last winter. Doctor Flint was sure you'd die!"

I never knew that Doctor Flint said that! 'It's just a chill,' was all he said to me. I'll never trust that ancient liar again.

"Well, Doctor Flint was wrong," I pointed out. "I'm fit and well now, as you see. Perhaps I'll live to ninety-three and show I'm stronger than I look!"

"But Miss," the girl went on, "your mother, Mrs Grey, would never let you go down there! She'd sooner lock you in the cellar and throw away the key!"

"My mother need not know. We'll go at night, when you have finished work downstairs," I said.

"But Cook would never let us go till midnight!" Molly gasped.

"Then midnight it will have to be. The streets will all be quiet by then, the taverns closed, the drunks gone home to bed. Is that not true?" I asked.

She nodded dumbly.

"Then", I said, "you bring some clothes – your own would fit me – and I will pay you." Still she stood and stared, quite tongue-tied. "If you won't help me then I'll go there on my own," I threatened. "Perhaps your home is not so bad as you've been saying. Perhaps you wouldn't want me seeing how you live in luxury!" I tried to joke, but still she stood and stared at me.

At last she moaned, "Oh, not at midnight, Miss! Oh, any time but then."

"And why not midnight? As I said it seems as safe a time as any – the villains all should be asleep!"

"But there's one kind of villain comes awake at midnight."

"What kind is that?"

"I dare not say."

"They live in Low Street?"

"Not in Low Street."

"Where then? Tell me, don't just stand there!"

"A place we'd have to pass to get to Low Street . . . a place quite close at hand." She swallowed hard. "The graveyard down the Walk!" she croaked.

I laughed. "If you mean ghosts, there's no such thing!"

"There's lights been seen," she breathed. "Blue lights, the kind they call corpse candles – they've seen them over fresh dug graves. I've seen them for myself!"

"Molly! What you're saying's sinful. You were in the church last Sunday, and you heard the vicar say that all good Christians go to heaven. The bad ones go to . . . the other place. But none – and he said none – would hang around a chilly graveyard just to scare the likes of you."

Molly's pretty face was serious when she said, "I know and I believed him, though I didn't want to."

"Didn't want to? But why not?"

"Because if they're not ghosts that flicker those corpse candles then they must be something worse!" she breathed.

"You mean to say there's worse things on this earth than ghosts?" I asked.

"Oh yes, Miss, things much worse."

"And what are they, pray?" I demanded, irritated by this nonsense.

Her lip was trembling and it was a minute before she found the courage to frame the words. "Please, Miss . . . the sack-'em-up men's worse!"

And then she fled before she'd told me what they were. I'd never heard the name before. It held no fear for me. And sack-'em-up or sack-'em-down, I wasn't going to let them stop me seeing *John* again.

For half that night I waited in the library and looked across the graveyard for some sign. But nothing moved except moon-shadows. Not one ghost and not one sack-'em-up . . . whatever they may be.

Next morning I was half exhausted, still determined that I'd get to Low Street at midnight. Father was in a filthy temper. After reading the news-sheet he became quite upset because some man had died down at the docks. "That's seven this week," he growled. "The corporation will enforce quarantine if we're not careful, and then where would we be?"

I shook my head. I hadn't any notion why my poor papa was getting so upset. But something drew me to my window late that afternoon and there I overlooked the funeral. A pauper's unmarked grave in the south-east corner of the graveyard.

I thought no more about it. I slept sound that afternoon and through till night when Molly woke me. "Eleven o'clock, Miss, you said you wanted waking . . . Oh, Miss, are you sure you want to go ahead with this mad scheme?"

"I do. You fetched some clothing?"

"Yes, Miss . . . and I hope you don't mind, Miss," she said shyly.

"What won't I mind?"

"I asked my brother John if he'd be good enough to meet us at the end of Manor Walk just as the church strikes midnight."

I didn't mind. Of course I didn't mind. I'd looked forward to the time when I could see her John again. Of course my sole concern was that he'd kept our bargain, never being late for work!

The dress was coarse and dreary woollen but at least quite clean – Molly's mother had washed it for a farthing. The ankle boots were strong and warm but not the supple leather that my feet are used to. I pulled a dark green knitted scarf around my head and dared to look into the mirror. I sighed. I didn't want to look too rich and be attacked, but I didn't want to look too plain if John was waiting down the walk. I pinned my best gold brooch on to my collar, but Molly made me take it off.

Somehow, though she was scared, she seemed more calm than me!

The house was almost silent. I could hear the ticking of a clock and mice scuttering on the ceiling boards.

We crept along the landing and I cursed my clumsy boots. The stairs, it seemed, had creaks in every tread. We had a lantern but we didn't dare light it till we reached the Walk outside.

We left the Grey Manor by the kitchen door leading into the garden where the cook grew vegetables, then crept along the path that ran beside the graveyard wall. The night was full of sounds. Alive.

Bats flapped among the rustling graveyard yews, cats cried to one another, somewhere down in Seawell dogs *began to bark. And then the midnight hour began to chime. I felt more thrilled than ever in my life!*

I tiptoed down the drive and out into the Walk and then we took the path past the graveyard railings.

The seventh stroke was sounding when I heard poor Molly gasp, "The lights! Corpse candles! See them burning – over there!"

She pointed to the south-east corner of the graveyard. Close to where they laid that man to rest that afternoon. I saw the pale blue lights that burned close to the ground.

I must confess I felt afraid. It's easy, when it's daylight, to say you're not afraid. But in that instant by the graveyard I believed in ghosts as sure as I believed in Molly standing next to me.

Suddenly a voice called, "Molly! Are you there?"

"Yes, John, we're here!" she cried and dragged me towards the corner. Even as I stumbled after her my eyes were fixed upon those lights. Then, with a clattering of metal and the soft cursing of voices, the lights went out!

"The ghosts have gone!" I said. "They're more afraid of us than we of them!" I laughed. But not a laugh of joy – a laugh of mad release.

"Oh, shush, Miss! Shush!" Molly moaned. "Not ghosts but sack-'em-up men like I warned! They'll chase us with pitch plasters if they can."

"Pitch plasters? What are they?" I asked, but Molly didn't answer.

John saw us tumble down the Walk and ran to meet us. I all but fainted in his arms. "Are you all right, Miss Grey?"

"Oh, hurry, John!" his sister cried.

"What's wrong?"

"Resurrectionists!" she moaned.

At that magic word John took charge. "Down this side alley!" he said softly and took my hand in his own thin, rough hand. He dragged me down a path between two buildings. Even the moon couldn't find us there. "Now silent! Try not to breathe!" he warned.

I realised that I was panting. I leaned against the cool stone wall and said, "But what are . . ."

"Later," he said. "If you want to live you must make no sound!"

The street beyond the alley was silent. I heard no one, yet something passed before the noon and cast two ragged shadows. My heart beat hard against my stays – my fault for making Molly lace them hard. The lightest breath of air brought a sickening smell of death to my nose . . . and then it was gone.

John breathed a sigh of relief. "They're gone. You're safe for now, Miss Grey," he murmured. "But, to be sure, I'll take you back to Grey Manor."

"You'll not!" I hissed. "Your sister promised that I'd go to your house. You can't go back on any promise."

"You're stubborn and you're mad, Miss Grey . . . if you don't mind my saying so."

"I certainly do mind," I snapped.

His grin showed even in the darkness. "Very well, you're stubborn and you're mad, Miss Grey . . . even if you do mind my saying so." I gave a sniff of disgust to show what I thought of his impertinence. "We'll go the back streets to make sure we don't meet them again," he said.

77

"*You may take my arm to guide me,*" I said coldly.

"*You're too kind,*" he said. I know he didn't mean it.

"*Molly,*" I said to the other figure in the shadow.

"*Yes, Miss?*"

"*Your brother needs some lessons in manners,*" I told her. She giggled. "*It isn't funny.*"

"*No, Miss, only that's what Mrs Grey said to Mr Grey about you just yesterday!*"

Her insolent brother, to my shame, joined in her laughter. Of course to be polite, you understand, I had to laugh myself.

We were in such a good humour I hardly noticed the tiresome journey, stumbling and slipping down the steep streets to the river bank. The dark was a blessing since it meant I couldn't see what I was stepping in, but I could smell it and that was enough to make me ill. Something squealed one time and wriggled underneath my boot. I gave a cry but John laughed, "*Just a rat!*"

I felt a little faint and leaned more on his arm. He slipped the arm around my waist, the better to support me. For such a thin boy he seemed to have a lot of strength. I do believe he enjoyed his arm around my waist! Father would have horse-whipped him had he known.

"*We're here, Miss Grey,*" he said at last. Molly had lit her lantern. We stood before a wooden house that smelled of the tar that covered father's ships. John pushed the flapping door and led me in.

The lantern showed a simple room, sawdust on the floor and beds of straw against the walls. A cauldron of foul-smelling liquid bubbled on a dying fire. Two heaps of clothes stirred on the straw – I made out they were people. "Dad's drunk again," John said.

"And Mother too," Molly added as she kicked an empty stone jar.

"So, this is where you live?" I asked.

John nodded. "Thanks to Mr Fawcett. He built these houses for his workers. If my dad doesn't get back to work soon we'll have to leave," he sighed.

"What then?"

"The workhouse, I suppose," he shrugged.

"But not if Billy gets home soon," his sister said. She turned to me. "Billy is our oldest brother. He went off to sea two years ago. He's due home soon. I'll bet he's made his fortune!"

"I hope so, Molly. If not, perhaps I'll talk to Father. I'm sure he'd find a better house for you and all your family!"

"No! Don't do that!" John cried. "We don't complain. We've seen what happens to families who complain. They end up out of jobs."

"My father wouldn't . . ." I began.

"He does it all the time. The Murphy family found that out," he said with bitterness.

I felt ashamed. I changed the topic of our talk. "Who are those men? The ones who haunt the graveyard?"

"Don't you know about the sack-'em-up men?" he asked. I shook my head. He edged a little nearer on the straw while Molly nodded sleepily. "The sack-'em-up men are Resurrectionists . . ."

"But what's a Resurrectionist?"

"Why, a body-snatcher, of course!"

"Of course," I said weakly.

"They take fresh corpses from the graves and sell them to the surgeons. Put them in sacks . . . they sack-'em up! The surgeons cut them up to learn how human bodies work," he said. His huge brown eyes were sombre – he wasn't lying. Yet still I could not believe them.

"They can't do that!" I argued.

"They do. A good fresh body earns them ten guineas or more – half a year's wages to folk like us."

"The constables should stop them."

"They've tried. But constables are men and men like money. They bribe the law to look the other way. Some families guard the graves for weeks until their kin are safe. Some bury coffins in steel cages to keep the body-snatchers out. It's sad, but greed is greed and money's hard come by."

"That's no excuse!" I cried. John's parents stirred and moaned. A rat ran past my foot. "That's no excuse," I said more softly. "You're poor," I said "but you'd not stoop to robbing graves!"

John's brown eyes sparkled in the lamplight and he looked at me. "Oh, no," he smiled. "The bodies I prefer are very much alive."

I'll swear I blushed a crimson shade of red. "I think you'd better take me home!"

"Of course!" he said. "But let's leave Molly sleeping," he added nodding at his softly snoring sister.

We went out in the cold night. Again he took my arm and led me through the shadowed alleys. My fears made the body-snatchers leap round every corner. I clung to

John as if to life. "If they'd seen us, those sack-'em-up men, what would they have done?" I asked.

"They have these plasters made of tar or pitch. They'd slap them round your mouth and nose to stop your screams," he said.

"I'd suffocate!" I shuddered.

"Yes. You would."

"I'd die!"

"That's true. And you be in their hands. That saves them digging up your corpse!"

"But that's not body-snatching!" I exclaimed.

"That's right. It's murder. All the same to them."

We'd passed the graveyard now and stood by Grey Manor kitchen door. "Miss Grey," John Brown said soberly, "Seawell's dangerous after dark. Stay here," he warned. "Your world is snug and safe. Stay here."

"It's boring, John," I sighed. "A skylark in a cage is snug and safe from catapults or cats, but it would swap that safety for an open door. So would I!"

He laughed that insolent, mocking laugh. The clock chimed one. "I'll have to go; mustn't over-sleep and be late for work."

"Thank you, John," I said and shook his hand. "Come and see me some time if you need help or money – come and see me! Will you?"

He didn't answer. "Goodnight, Miss Grey."

"Call me Marie."

"Goodnight, Miss Grey," he laughed and vanished.

I trust he's safe and well. More well than I am with this chill my night adventure cost me. But it was worth it, John. I now know what I must do with my life. Thank you, John.

Chapter Seven

Jamie was shaken by Marie's grim story. He feared for her in her brutal world and felt so helpless that he could do nothing to help her.

He hurried past the graveyard, grateful that he was early this evening and that there was enough light to keep the shadows from hiding secrets.

Trish had been disturbed too. Perhaps that was why she'd been so quiet this evening, or perhaps she remembered his cruel remarks from the previous night. Of course she might just have been heeding her father's warning not to become involved with him. Whatever the reason, it made him miserable.

He pushed his hands deep into his anorak pockets and trudged the streets with head down and deep in thought. He was so wrapped in gloom that he scarcely noticed the police car as it drove away from his brother's house.

Rob was standing at his door, watching the car disappear round the corner. Jamie sensed trouble. His brother leaned against the doorpost and seemed too dejected and tired to go back into the house. Jamie began to run.

"Rob? Rob!" he cried as he hurried down the path. "What's wrong? What's happened?"

Rob waved a weary hand at the house behind him. "Burgled," he said simply.

The brothers went into the house. The floor was a mess of books and papers and broken ornaments; the shelves and drawers were emptied. The chair cushions were scattered and pictures torn down from the walls.

"When did this happen?" Jamie asked.

"Mrs Bell next door saw my back door open at five, thought I was back early and called for a chat. She found this and called the police. She was certain the door wasn't open when she went to the shops at four."

"Has much been taken?"

"Portable TV and video, cassette recorder and tapes. There was no money in the house. If there had been some to find they might not have ripped the place apart looking for it."

Jamie nodded. They were certainly looking for something. "Come on, Rob, I'll help you tidy up." He began by picking up some of his brother's collection of rare history books and slotting them back on their shelves. By nine they were finished and sitting down with coffee – tired, but a bit more cheerful.

"So, kid, how's the History project going?" Rob asked.

"It's fascinating," Jamie said. "We're no closer to finding the treasure, mind."

"You didn't tell me this was a treasure hunt!"

"It is for Trish. Her father's sure that Joshua Grey left buried treasure. He wants to find it."

Rob lit his pipe and sucked at it noisily till it came to life. "I'm afraid Trish's father, Edward Grey, is not a good historian . . ."

"He knows so much about the Grey family, you wouldn't believe it!" Jamie objected.

"Knowledge is useless by itself. I know my house was burgled this evening, but that doesn't help me find who did it. The police have to go away and collect as many facts as they can, sort through them and come to some conclusion. A lot of those clues will be unimportant, but buried in that haystack of unimportant clues will be a few straws of truth. History's like that – sifting through the hay to find the truth."

"I know that," Jamie said, "but how does that make Mr Grey a bad historian?"

Rob waved the point of his pipe at his brother. "Edward Grey starts off with the answers. He only seeks the facts that prove his answers and he ignores the ones that don't fit his pattern. Remember, I knew him in the local history society before I went to university."

"How can he do that?" Jamie asked.

"You say he knows about the Grey family. How?"

"He studied the family library," Jamie said.

"All of it?"

"Well . . . yes!"

"Marie Grey's diary?"

"Not exactly – he looked at it. But surely all those details about body-snatchers can't be an important clue in hidden treasure!" Jamie argued.

"They could be the most important clue of all or they could be totally unimportant, but unless you have those facts to play with you'll never know! And he hasn't studied the local parish registers. I know because I did on my way home tonight. The vicar said that I was the first to examine them in years. And I'll bet he hasn't read the newspapers of the period. Joshua Grey was an important man – I'll bet he was mentioned a hundred times if he was mentioned once!"

"So you don't think he's right?" Jamie asked, a little disappointed.

Rob thumped the table, exasperated. "Of course he could be right! What I'm saying is that if you look for proofs inside your own front door you get a distorted picture!" He jumped to his feet and disappeared into the kitchen. A minute later he came out carrying his find. "Know what that is?" he asked.

"Of course," Jamie said. "It's a spirit level – shows if walls and things are truly flat."

Rob placed it on the hearth of his fireplace. "What does that tell you?"

"It tells me the hearth is level."

"It may tell *you* that!" Rob cried excitedly. "But I'm some mediaeval scientist. It tells *me* that the Earth is flat!"

"That's crazy!"

"Not to the mediaeval scientist! It's the men who argued that the world was a sphere who were called crazy – they were tortured until they denied it. But what they'd done was to go beyond the spirit level. They made telescopes and looked at the universe. They had to look at the stars to find the truth about their earth. Nothing is unimportant when you're searching for the truth."

"But Edward Grey is starting to look at other things. He wants that diary back now," Jamie said, remembering the purpose of his visit.

Rob picked up the spirit level and took it back to the kitchen. "That's interesting. I wonder why?"

"I don't know. On Monday he gave it to me but on Tuesday, yesterday, he was going crackers to get it back."

"What happened between him giving it you and him wanting it back?" Rob asked.

"Nothing," Jamie shrugged.

"Oh, but it did! Perhaps you know what happened, but it's one of those clues you overlooked because it didn't seem important at the time."

"Nothing happened that *I* know of," Jamie argued, "but the fact is he wants it back.

"Are you going to give it back?" Rob asked.

"But . . ." Jamie spluttered, "of course!"

"I haven't finished transcribing it. I've just finished the first half." He pulled open his briefcase. "Here's the latest section, hot off the word-processor," he went on, waving the papers at his brother.

"He'll be furious if I don't return it tonight!"

Rob squinted at the clock. "Half-nine now. Too late tonight. If I take tomorrow off work – tell them I'm clearing up after the burglary, sorting out insurance – they'll understand. I could be finished by tomorrow evening!"

Jamie stared into the dregs of his coffee cup and strained to remember something. "He said . . . he said that he didn't want someone like you having the secret of his treasure!"

Rob slid his hand into the briefcase and pulled out Marie Grey's leatherbound book. "In that case I just have to finish it!" he said with an eager twinkle in his eye.

"So you believe in the treasure too?" Jamie asked.

"I'll study *all* the facts and then decide," his brother said.

"Trish and I reckoned Joshua Grey gambled it all away."

"Just about impossible," Rob said briskly.

"And we reckoned that Marie had run away with someone unsuitable. That's why she wasn't mentioned in the will," Jamie went on.

Rob smiled. "There are other reasons why she might not be mentioned in the will," Rob said. "You're still working on the flat-Earth principle. You'd like to think she ran off with John Brown . . ."

"You what?" Jamie gasped.

"You'd like to think a girl like that could go off with someone unsuitable her father wouldn't approve of."

"But why would I think that?" Jamie laughed uncomfortably.

"Because if Marie Grey could defy her family and go off with John Brown, then anything's possible. Trish Grey could defy her father and go off with Jamie Williams!"

"What makes you think I even fancy her?" Jamie exploded.

"You don't?" his brother teased.

"I didn't say that!"

"You do, then?"

"What's that got to do with treasure?" he mumbled.

"Everything and nothing. It means that you're as bad as Edward Grey – desperate to find that treasure. Impress your Trish and be her hero. You're so desperate that you overlook the obvious truths! The facts that are staring you in the face when you read Marie's diary."

"You know what happened to her?" Jamie asked. "Tell me, Rob!"

His brother shook his head. "You have to look outside. Marie lived in a closed little world, but her father didn't."

"Her father hardly comes into her story," Jamie objected.

"No," Rob said, "but when he does it's significant."

"You know the answer!" Jamie cried.

"I have an idea, but I have to put it out of my mind, otherwise I'll try to prove my theory rather than seek for the whole truth," Rob explained.

"But tell me!"

"You have to find out for yourself," Rob said quietly. "Why not stay here tonight? I'll phone our mum and tell her where you are. Read this latest transcription before you go to bed."

Jamie was exasperated. He reached for the leather book. Marie's book. The girl with blue-velvet eyes. The doorbell rang.

"I'll get it," he said to Rob, who was on the phone.

He opened the front door and took a surprised step back. "What are you doing here?" he asked sharply.

"I've come to see your big brother, Williams." Eric Gott stepped into the light of the hallway and smiled. Jamie noticed he was alone.

Rob put the phone down and called, "Who is it?"

"Eric Gott!"

Gott pushed past Jamie and walked into the living room. "Call me Rick! Hello, Mr Williams."

Rob looked at him carefully. "Pinched any wheel-trims lately, Eric? As I remember that's what you were doing last time we met. What can I do for you?"

Gott seemed happy to forget the last time they met. "We've got this Humanities teacher, Mr Waites. Jamie might have told you about him."

"Jamie didn't have to tell me anything. Mr Waites used to be my teacher when I went to Seawell Comp. ten years ago. One of the best teachers I ever met."

"Oh, yeah," Gott sniffed. "Me and the lads think he's great. That's why we're so keen to do a good project for him."

"Very commendable," Rob said. "Sit down, Eric."

"Call me Rick."

"Sit down, Rick."

Gott's eyes flickered round the room, taking in every detail. He perched on the front edge of a red-leather armchair. "Mr Waites said we should go to as many sources as possible, not just books and museums and places but people as well. I come to ask what *you* know, seeing as how they reckon you're the expert on local history around here. You know everything there is to know!"

Rob was too wise to be taken in by the boy's attempt at flattery, but he just smiled and said, "I tend to specialise – Georgian period."

"Oh, yeah, Georgian period," Gott said and scratched his greasy hair. "Er, when's that then?"

"Roughly 1760 to 1830," Rob explained.

"Spot on, Mr Williams . . . just what I want!"

"And what's that?"

"Eh?"

"What is it that you want?"

"Eh? Oh! I can't say. It's secret!" the boy said letting his eyes stray to Jamie.

"Then I can't help you," Rob said. "Not if you won't tell me what it is."

"Nah, it's just that I didn't want the rest of the class to know . . . not till we hit them with it in the lesson. Know what I mean?" Gott grinned.

"No," Rob said flatly. "Jamie won't say anything, will you?"

Jamie shook his head. "Not even to your little girlfriend?" Gott sneered.

"She's not my girlfriend," Jamie growled.

Rob cut in. "Look, Eric, tell me the problem, with Jamie here, or go home. It's getting late."

"All right, chief . . ." He took a deep breath. "What do you know about . . . body-snatching?"

Rob's eyes narrowed. "Quite a bit happened in this area. Not organised gangs like they had in London, Edinburgh and Glasgow, but quite a lot. And most of it in the Georgian period. Funny, but I've just been doing some notes that mentioned body-snatching." Jamie knew he meant Marie Grey's diary. He glanced anxiously at the table where the book had lain when he went to the door. He remembered Gott's interest in the book. The book had disappeared.

Gott was a skilled thief, but he hadn't had a chance to take it. Rob must have hidden it before the visitor came into the room. And now he was asking Gott, "What do you need to know?"

"Well, we've read some books, and we've had a look at the old graveyard, of course," he said, pleased with himself.

"So that's what you were doing there the other night?" Jamie murmured.

"Right. But old Waites is keen on what he calls alec-totes," Gott said, stumbling over an unfamiliar word.

"Alec who?" Rob asked, raising one eyebrow in amusement.

"Stories that people told about what really happened," Gott said.

Rob nodded. "Anecdotes."

"Yeah. That's what I said. Alec-totes. Anyway, we thought you're the man to ask. So?" Gott said eagerly.

"So?"

"So, you *got* any stories? Liven up our presentation no end. We might even turn them into a play."

"Dramatise them?"

"Yeah. That 'n' all!"

Rob rose and searched the bookshelves. "I do have a book – usually know where every one is . . ." he said running his finger along the spines. "But they've all been disturbed."

"Yeah, shame about that," Gott sniffed.

"Shame about what, Eric?" Rob said casually.

The boy twitched. "Shame about the burglary."

"You know?"

"Oh, yeah! Saw the police car. Just live in the next street, you know. Lot of villains around. Want to get a burglar alarm fitted, Mr Williams."

Rob turned from the shelves. "How do you know I *don't* have an alarm?" he said quietly.

Gott shifted uncomfortably on the edge of his seat. "Stands to reason, Mr Williams," he said with a flickering attempt at a grin.

"And what made you think the books would be disturbed?" Rob asked mildly.

"Stands to reason," Gott said again.

"You have a good sense of reason, Eric. You'd

make a good historian – or policeman, perhaps. I'm sure you'd solve the crime in no time," Rob said.

Gott laughed a loud, hearty and totally false laugh. "You're a one, Mr Williams! You're a real joker, you are."

The historian pulled a book from the shelf and thumbed through it. "Here we are," he said, pointing to a page. "You want to make notes?"

"Eh? What? Oh, no. Keep it all in my computer-like brain!" the boy joked.

"The best story is about a sailor from a Seawell's ship," Rob lowered his voice. Jamie knew he was going to make the history come to life. Gott sat forward and his mouth hung loosely open. "It was a foggy winter night and the sailor was staggering home from the inns of Low Street. He'd had an upsetting day. That afternoon he'd been to the funeral of his mate, Geordie, who'd died while they were at sea. He turned to go down Queen Street. He thought he'd visit the piemen's stall to get a bite of supper, but all was silent."

Rob paused. Gott's eyes were bulging. Rob let him hear the silence. "The market was closed," he went on, even softer. "The piemen's charcoal oven was cold. No shrill voices calling, 'Chelsea buns! Pies all smoking hot! Hot mutton pies!' So he turned back homeward. Past the 'kitty' – that was a prison cell at the foot of Crown Street, where some poor freezing criminal was moaning to the midnight air – and into Manor Walk. Past the church. Then past the grave-yard. Then he stopped. He rubbed his hand across his eyes, because he couldn't believe what he was seeing."

"What did he see, Mr Williams? What did he see?" Gott croaked.

"Something white appeared to be climbing over the railings, out of the churchyard."

Jamie gulped despite himself and said, "What was it?"

"The sailor went closer. Someone was hanging awkwardly over the top of those railings! 'What are ye doing there?' he called drunkenly. He got no reply. He stepped closer . . . and found himself looking into the face of his old mate, Geordie! He grabbed the corpse's hand to see if it was real. 'Here, Geordie, yer cold,' he said. 'Better get back in your coffin!'"

Gott gave a nervous snigger. "Is all this true?"

But Rob went on, "Suddenly the body vanished. It had been hauled back over the railings by some hands that were hidden in the fog. The sailor set off down the lane and reached the sexton's house – that's the man who looked after the graveyard. 'Better get up!' he cried. 'The dead 'uns are getting out of the churchyard!' But by the time they examined the grave they found the soil disturbed, the body gone. Only the grave clothes were left!"

"And did they catch the body-snatchers?" Gott asked.

"That's the strangest part of the story. Six bodies vanished in as many weeks. So guards were set at graveyards. They were so nervous they shot at anything that moved – once they shot a pig near

Aberdeen! But the body-snatchers must have found it too dangerous to work in Seawell. A graveyard guard fired at two shadows lurking in Manor Walk one night. He swore they looked just like the piemen who worked in the market. Said he'd ask them next time he saw them. But next day they were seen boarding the coach for Edinburgh. And three years later they *were* heard of again – arrested in Edinburgh for robbing graves and murder. They became the most famous body-snatchers in history – Burke and Hare."

"I've heard of them!" Gott said excitedly. "And those two operated in Seawell?" he asked. "What a story, Mr Williams!"

Rob rose to his feet and went to the door. Gott followed a little reluctantly. "Ah, just one more thing, Mr Williams. Jamie said you have this diary that he's working on . . . Mr Waites wants me to look at it . . . Jamie said it's all right if you just give it to me."

"Sorry, left it at the university," Rob lied and hustled the reluctant boy out of the door.

Back in the living room, Rob pulled the diary from his briefcase. "First he breaks into the house and tears my home half apart looking for it; then, when he can't find it, he comes round and brazenly asks for it. I wonder why?" He opened the book. "I'll work on it now."

"And I'll read the last part," Jamie said, pulling the sheets towards him.

Chapter Eight

[Some of the events that Marie mentions here are a matter of historical record. I've therefore been able to date the events to the second week of October 1831 – Rob.]

And now I'm turned to body-snatching! But, like John Brown, the bodies I prefer are very much alive!

It began with my first morning down to breakfast after my chill. Of course old Doctor Flint said that I should not be out of bed, but I was so bored with staying in my room. I think I've now read every novel ever written.

Papa was in perhaps the worst mood I have ever seen him. "Another man has died in Queen Street," he sighed. "That makes the total ten . . . no doubt the council will act."

"It's not like you to get yourself upset over the death of one of the poor," The Old Besom said. And that was true.

"Caroline," he said sternly, "you women are not aware of the background or the implications of these deaths. You live up here in Grey Manor and know nothing of the world outside." And that reminded me of what John Brown had said when last I saw him.

"Perhaps, my dear, we'd know some more if you were kind enough to tell us," she said in her voice as sweet as steel.

"It isn't pleasant," father muttered.

"Perhaps we women have more strength than you might give us credit for," my mother said as she piled his plate with scrambled egg and kidney.

"Well, I have anyway," dear sister Lou said spitefully. "Unlike Marie who's weaker than this tea. I think Cook should be dismissed."

"Be quiet, Louise, and listen to Papa," The Old Besom snapped. "Now, Joshua, tell us all about this man who passed on to a better life."

"It couldn't be to a worse life. I've seen the slums of Low Street – ugh!" Louise sniffed.

Father wiped his mouth on his cotton napkin. "The man who died was called Jack Crawford . . ."

"I've heard of him!" The Besom cried.

"That's right," my father nodded. "Hero of the last French wars!"

"What did he do?" I asked, excited, loving tales of war and daring men.

"He sailed upon the flagship of the fleet. One day

they came across the French. The French fired first. They snapped the mainmast of Jack's ship. The flag – the flag that led the fleet – came tumbling to the deck. A great disaster. The English ships had nothing they could follow. It meant defeat for sure! The admiral saw that someone had to take the flag and nail it to the foremast.''

"That's easy,'' Lou scoffed. "Anyone can climb a silly pole.''

"It's harder when the French are firing down a rain of cannonball and musket shot,'' reproved my father. "The man who climbed that mast would have to have a special kind of courage. 'I want a volunteer!' the admiral cried above the raging sound of cannon. No man stepped forward. So cabin boy, Jack Crawford, one of Seawell's finest sons, stepped up and took the flag. 'I'll go!' he said, and off he set to climb the mast . . . this tea is really weak – perhaps the cook should go, my dear.''

"Never mind the tea, Papa! What about brave Jack?'' I urged.

"The French saw Crawford climbing up the mast, of course. They turned their every gun upon him. Musket shot tore at his clothes but, being English, God was on his side of course. He reached the top, he nailed the flag and reached the deck unharmed. The English won the fight and Jack became a Seawell hero. There was some talk of building him a statue that could stand on Mowbray Hill.''

"And now he's died?'' I asked.

"And now he's died,'' my father nodded.

"I thought you said that God was on his side,'' my sister sneered.

"A sinful thing to say," my mother snapped but said no more. Louise is her great pet.

"He can't have been that old," I said.

"Just thirty-one," Papa replied. "The illness takes them every age."

"What illness, father?"

"Cholera," he said. Not an illness I've heard of before. "It grips the bowels and causes cramps and sickness. Death is sure within a day – the corpse is left a horrid shade of blue!"

My mother screamed. "Oh, Joshua, must you? Please! Not at the breakfast table."

He reached across to pat her hand. "Of course, my dear, but you did ask!"

"To know why these deaths should upset you," she explained.

"Because it can be bad for business," Father sighed.

"Oh, no!" The Old Besom gasped and gripped his shaking hand.

"Today, I know the council will issue a proclamation. Macmillan's on the council and he told me of their plans. They'll say that cholera is brought to Seawell on the ships that come from other countries. The only way to stop it is to impose a quarantine."

"What's that?" Lou asked.

"It means, my dear, that ships that come to Seawell must wait outside the harbour for perhaps ten days or more. They won't be let into our port until they've proved a healthy crew."

"A good idea," Louise sniffed. "We don't want half of Seawell turning blue. It's not my favourite colour!"

"Be quiet, brat!" my father thundered. "You cannot see how bad this is for trade. The goods out on the ships will rot if they're left out ten days unloaded. I've paid a fortune for those cargoes but some will not be worth a penny! Then my coal is coming from the mines and no empty ships are ready to transport it! The mines will have to close or I'll lose money, paying men to work for coal that can't be sold. For us this is disaster!"

"And what about the poor who live in danger down in Low Street?" I asked, fearing for dear John. "Shouldn't they be shielded from this cholera by a quarantine on all ships?"

My father turned on me in fury. "Sometimes, child, you make me wonder just whose side you're on!" My sister giggled, seeing Father's favourite being snapped at in this way. My tongue was tied. Papa went on, "The dockside poor deserve their fate. They live in filth and filth will breed disease. They need good food but they prefer to spend their money on cheap gin. Or rather they prefer to spend my money. For I make the money that pays them. And if Apollo can't get in I'll have no money."

"Does Apollo work for you, Papa?" Lou asked sweetly.

"No, no, no, child. I mean Grey Apollo that's my finest ship. She's due home now and Captain Carter has the money earned from near two years at sea. A bankers' draft is on that ship for seven thousand pounds! Think of all that we could buy for seven thousand pounds! Think of seven thousand pounds just floating, useless, in the North Sea."

"Can you do nothing, dearest?" The Old Besom asked.

"I could row out to Apollo when she arrives, but I'd risk being held in quarantine myself. Or I could pay a thousand pounds in bribes and have the council change its mind," he said gloomily. "Last time I rowed out past the harbour I was sicker than a dog."

"And a thousand pounds is far too much to pay in bribes. You paid three hundred just last month to hush the mine inspectors," Mother said, disgusted.

Father rose. "I'll find some way," he said. He ruffled up my hair, our quarrel quite forgotten. "Take care, my treasure," he said. "Wrap up well and nurse that chill!"

I went up to my room, but not to nurse my chill. I called for Molly and I asked her how they fared on Low Street.

"Shocked we were when poor Jack Crawford died – we're all afraid," she said. "The church was full last Sunday, people praying they'd be safe from this disease. Collection plates were full to overflowing."

"Oh, Molly, they don't think they'll buy God's favours by giving to collections?" I laughed.

But Molly's face was serious as she said, "Why not, Miss? The rich folk of the town give so much every week and you never see rich people dying from the cholera!"

And she was right. Grey Manor lay beside the graveyard yet was never touched by death.

"And how's your brother?" I asked, hoping for some news of John.

"Our Billy isn't back yet," Molly said. Then she spent hours telling me about her older brother. Fine and *handsome, clever too. How he'd sailed the world, made a fortune and would bring it home to Low Street. At last she stopped for breath.*

"And John?" I asked.

"Oh, John is never late for work these days. He says he owes the job to you – he cannot let you down!"

"And does he talk about me, Molly?"

"Oh, all the time, Miss. Father says – or when he's sober Father says – that John has lost his heart to you."

"Molly!"

"But Mother says he may as well lose his heart to the moon, he has as much chance of holding it," she added sadly.

I'll swear I blushed redder than a rose. A fit of coughing meant I couldn't talk for half an hour or more – perhaps just as well.

But next day Molly woke me, all excitement. "Oh Miss, oh Miss!" she cried. "I have a letter here for you!"

I yawned and stretched. My chest was aching with the chill, but I sat up. "A letter, Molly? Is it from Emma?"

"Oh, no Miss, no. It's a letter from our John!"

"From John!" I gasped. "But John can't write!"

Molly blushed with pride and told me how he'd learnt when he was young from some old woman in Queen Street. And now he was the only man in Low Street who could read and write.

I took the letter. "You may leave now, Molly," I said, but she looked so disappointed that I said, "No, stay and light my fire."

"Yes, Miss," she grinned and busied herself at my hearth while I opened the letter.

"Miss Grey," John said . . . I wish he'd call me Marie. "The other night you said that I must see you if I needed help." Yes, I remembered. "And now the family has a problem. I can think of no one else to turn to. My father lost his job at Fawcett's shipyard – his illness made him miss some days." The illness is called 'gin', I thought. "And now the Fawcetts say we have to leave their house in Low Street. The worker taking father's job needs to have a place to live. We'll have to move into some lodging house or sleep out in the street. We must move out today. The keeper of the lodging house wants one month's money in advance. A guinea we don't have."

I thought that John was going to ask if I could lend some money. I was wrong, of course. My John is much too proud to beg. "Our Billy's ship, Apollo, reached home late last night. We know he has a fortune in his purse that would buy a dozen lodging houses. Alas, Miss Grey, he finds he's trapped upon the ship. The council has enforced a quarantine and he must stay for fourteen days. And where are we to live those fourteen days?"

So, Father isn't the only one damaged by this law, I thought. Poor John!

"Your father is a powerful man, Miss Grey. I'm sure that he could find a way to break the quarantine and contact Billy on the ship."

I shook my head. If Father knew a way then he'd find it, and it would be seven thousand pounds and not some poor sailor's purse that he'd aim to save.

"If you could keep us from the poorhouse then I'd be forever grateful, dear Miss Grey," he concluded. "Your humble servant, John Brown."

I pressed the letter to my heart . . . until I noticed foolish Molly watching with a grin. "Your brother writes well," I said with dignity. "You know what's in the letter?" I asked.

"Oh, no, Miss . . . John wouldn't tell us. Said it's private."

"Quite right!" I approved of John. "But I can share some of the letter with you – not the intimate parts, of course."

"Oh, no, Miss!" Molly breathed and sat down at the end of my bed, eyes wide.

"It seems you need to contact Billy on Apollo?" Molly nodded, silent. "And no one may leave the ships nor anyone go near them for at least two weeks?"

"They're not supposed to, Miss, but of course it's hard for them to stop rich, important ladies of the town."

"Why would important ladies want to go near the ships?" I asked.

"Oh, Miss, you've been up here in bed. You haven't heard, have you?"

"How could I?" I asked impatiently.

"Yesterday the council announced its quarantine. But the Seawell Ladies Charitable Society insisted that the sailors couldn't be left to rot out on the edge of the harbour for two weeks. They said the sailors must be taken fresh fruit to fight the scurvy, fresh water and Bibles to read."

"Bibles?"

"Yes, Miss. Bibles," she said. "To keep their minds occupied!"

"Very noble," I said and wondered what the sailors would say to a box of Bibles arriving on the ship. "Did the council approve?"

"Oh, no, Miss! But Mrs Fawcett – your friend Emma's mother – said the council wouldn't dare to stop her. She said that God would send a sea serpent to sink the pilot if he tried to stop her!"

I nodded. "I'd rather face a sea serpent than an angry Mrs Fawcett any day."

Suddenly my plan began to form. "When are they going?" I asked.

"This afternoon, Miss."

"Then we are going to form the Seawell Young Ladies Charitable Society this afternoon and visit Grey Apollo!"

"You're not well, Miss Grey!" Molly argued and wrung her hands. "Your father won't allow it!"

"My father will send me with his blessing," I told her, throwing my bedclothes back and feeling better than I had for a week. "Pack my old brown woollen dress with petticoats and shawl in a bag, then put a Bible on top of it."

Molly looked bewildered but didn't dare question my orders. While she set about packing a bag I hurried downstairs to catch Papa before he left for his office. I quickly told him my plan.

"Marie, my child!" he said. "You are a treasure. Brilliant idea. Be at the dock by noon and I'll have the boat ready."

"And an oarsman," I reminded him.

"Of course."

"Perhaps you could send Molly's brother, John Brown. He'd be willing to help since it's his brother on the ship."

"That young scoundrel!"

"Please, Papa!" I smiled.

"Oh, very well!" Suddenly he put his arm around my shoulder. *"You'll be the saving of this family yet!"* His crushing hug brought on my painful cough. *"You'll wrap up well against the sea mist, won't you?"*

I assured him that I would and he left to make the arrangements for my trip. Meanwhile I wrote letters to all of my friends – the plan depended on there being a crowd of us. My friends, game for adventure too, did not let me down. By noon there were nine of us, including Molly, assembled by the dock. I believe we made more noise than the crate of geese that were being loaded on Grey Pride! The dock workers had certainly never seen anything like it before. Emma Fawcett swore that John Brown was the best-looking dock worker she'd ever seen. I told her, of course, that I was utterly shocked by her improper thought. Secretly I agreed with her.

It took about half an hour to row out to Grey Apollo. An officer in the pilot's boat warned us that we were breaking the quarantine. I stood up like Lord Nelson in command of my small craft. *"Sir,"* I said, *"my father owns that ship. I will die for my right to board my own family's ship."*

My friends cheered, but the man was clearly embarrassed. *"Please, Miss. It's my duty to warn you that you could help bring death into Seawell."*

"A Grey ship would never carry cholera," I said proudly. "Row on, Brown!" I ordered John.

The officer shook his head sadly. Even John looked unhappy.

But minutes later we were boarding Grey Apollo. The girls set about distributing fruit and Bibles to bewildered sailors, while I sought out Captain Carter.

"Miss Grey," he said severely, "a ship is no place for young ladies."

"Captain, I come with an urgent message from my father. He wants you to send the banker's draft ashore with a trusty man . . . he wants you to send Billy Brown."

Captain Carter shook his head. "The patrol would let you ladies go ashore, but never one of my men. He would be shot on sight."

"Let me see Billy Brown and I will explain my plan."

The captain led us below deck to some stinking cabin. Molly rushed to her brother and it took some mintues to separate her and hush her before I was introduced. Billy looked much like John: the same amused brown eyes, but an older and stronger man. "So, how do I get ashore?" he asked. "Preferably alive!"

"You dress in my old dress," I told him. "Molly, you have it in the bag." She took it out and showed him. Billy shrugged and said, "I suppose it would be better than two weeks stuck here with my home in sight after two years away, but, still . . ."

"Then hurry," I urged.

He shook his head. "I have a friend, Joseph. He's not

feeling too well. He needs me to look after him. Really he needs a doctor. I cannot leave him.'' Billy pointed to a small bundle in the corner of the dingy cabin where a man lay breathing shallowly and looking feverish. Suddenly a picture came to me of my last night's adventure. The sack-'em-up men!

''Take him ashore in a sack!'' I said. ''We'll say it's a bundle of washing John's taking to his mother for the crew.''

''It will never work,'' Billy argued.

''Never!'' Molly agreed. But she helped make the poor man comfortable in a sack. With Billy squeezed into my woollen dress and shawl, John threw the sack over his shoulder, and we climbed back into the rowing boat. My friends were confused to see the sailor in a dress but took it in the true spirit of the adventure. The patrol had not thought to count the crowd of girls in the boat and let us return with no comment.

By two o'clock we were ashore again. Billy brought money for his family and took Joseph to the poorhouse hospital, and I brought a banker's draft for seven thousand pounds! In one afternoon I saved two families and had more adventure than any heroine in any book I've ever read.

But being a heroine, I must admit, has exhausted me. I have slept for a day and a half before finding the strength to write this. I must try to get up now. I promised Billy that I'd visit his friend, Joseph, in the hospital. Perhaps I can help him too. My life has been so barren here in Grey Manor. Helping those in need makes it seem so much more worthwhile.

Chapter Nine

Jamie hurried into school just before the bell rang for morning classes. He caught Trish as she was going through the door into her registration room. "Trish, I . . ." he began. "You all right?"

Her face was unusually pale, even for Trish. Almost transparent. Her eyes were wide and scared. "Jamie," she said quietly.

"What is it?"

"The diary . . ."

"Yes, I have another part here," he said, pulling the sheets out of his pocket. "I think I can see where the Grey fortune may have gone!" he went on eagerly. "The cholera outbreak in 1831 could have bankrupted Joshua Grey. Marie saved him seven thousand pounds, but if it went on too long he could have been in serious trouble . . ."

"Oh," Trish said wearily.

"Trish? Aren't you interested any more? In the project? In what happened to the Grey fortune?" he asked. So much time and work and now she didn't care? He felt betrayed.

"Oh, yes," she said softly.

"Then what's wrong?"

"The diary," she said. Her deep blue eyes were troubled.

"I have it here," he said, waving the sheets. "Rob will be finished decoding the last part today," he promised.

"But the original. I have to have the original," she said urgently.

He stepped back a pace. "You too? What's so special about the original? Your father went crazy when I didn't return it, then Rob's house was broken into last night. He reckoned someone was trying to steal the diary!"

"Steal it!" she cried. "They didn't steal it, did they?" She was so distressed that the others in the classroom turned to stare. Jamie pulled her sleeve and led her into the corridor.

"They didn't steal it," he assured her. "Rob reckons it was Eric Gott who . . ."

Trish's head jerked up. "Gott! Yes. It would be. He didn't get it, did he?"

Jamie took her hand. She didn't seem to notice. "Look, I told you, the diary's safe with Rob . . . so what's it all about? Why do they all want the diary?"

The girl looked at him carefully. "You don't know?" she asked.

"Of course not! I've found one or two clues about where the Grey fortune went – Joshua's gambling or the cholera epidemic may have lost it, but there's no buried treasure!"

"But there is!" she said. "And we have to find it before Gott and his friends!"

"What's happened since I saw you last night?" Jamie asked.

A teacher rounded the corner of the corridor and Trish dropped Jamie's hand self-consciously. "See me after school – school library!" she said and vanished into the room.

The rest of that day was misery for Jamie. He felt that most of the pieces of the jigsaw were there, but Gott held some and he held others while Trish and her father held others still. And why was she now so sure that there was Grey treasure hidden somewhere?

He spent the lunch break re-reading Marie Grey's dairy and feeling depressed. As Rob had said he could see now where the story of Marie was going. He'd need a lot of nerve to read the last part. Just before afternoon school he phoned Rob.

"Have you finished decoding it?"

"Yes, just ten minutes ago," Rob said.

"And?"

"And what?"

"And is there any clue about treasure?"

Rob laughed. "I always said there was no treasure,

Jamie!" He sensed his younger brother's disappointment over the phone. "Look, I have to visit the archives this afternoon. I should have the final answer then. But Marie's last entry just about sealed it for me. Oh, by the way, Jamie . . ."

"Yes?"

"Did you give me everything? I mean, there isn't another sheet of paper missing, is there? It could be important, but I doubt it."

"I don't understand," Jamie said.

"At the back of Marie's book there are a couple of loose sheets of paper. Seem to have been pasted in. But the paste has lost its strength over the years. The last page doesn't make complete sense. Seems as if there should be another, final sheet. You haven't got it, have you?"

"No," Jamie said.

"Never mind, probably not important. See you later!"

"See you!"

Jamie was already in the library when Trish came in after school. She looked more relaxed and managed a smile when she saw him sitting at the library table. Some of the warmth began to flow between them again.

"You all right?" he asked.

"Fine. Sorry if I was a bit dramatic this morning. I'd had a couple of shocks."

"Tell me."

"I was making breakfast this morning when Father came into the kitchen. He asked if I'd seen you last night, and I said I had. He asked why you hadn't brought the diary back and I explained. I also asked him why he was so keen to see the diary. He wouldn't look me in the eye. Said something about it being a family heirloom, valuable antique, and so on. Then he let slip that he felt it would help solve the mystery of the treasure. I told him we'd read the transcripts and worked out that there was no treasure."

Jamie nodded. "What did he say to that?"

"He became agitated, the way he was the other night. Said he could *prove* that there was treasure. I wanted to see the proof and I decided the best way was to scoff at the idea."

"Make him annoyed enough to show you? Did it work?"

She went thoughtful for a moment. The memory was still too fresh and painful. "Sometimes I think he's mad, Jamie." She looked up. "I mean insane. He went straight to his desk drawer and took out a sheet of old paper. He pushed it under my nose and told me to read it."

"A piece of paper that had fallen out of the diary?" Jamie asked.

"How did you know?"

"Never mind now. Tell me what it said."

"It said . . ." she closed her eyes to try and picture the words. "It said, ' . . . and that is where we buried our treasure tonight. Safe from the evil, grasping hands that would desecrate the most perfect treasure any family ever had.' And a date: 'First day of November in the year of our Lord, Eighteen Hundred and Thirty-one.'"

Jamie sat back. "But *why*? Why bury their treasure, for goodness' sake?"

"Perhaps the first part of the letter would tell us . . . of course Father isn't too bothered about *why*! He only wants to know *where*!"

"And he found this sheet after I'd left? And that's why he wants the diary back, to see the first sheet that goes with it?"

Trish shook her head. "Not exactly. It seems you dropped the sheet in the street."

Jamie thumped the table and earned a glare from the teacher on duty in the library. "Of course! I ran into Gott and his friends prowling round the grave-yard! They threw the diary around a bit before I grabbed it back. It must have fallen out then!"

Trish nodded slowly. "I think Gott must have taken it to Father. My father was his solicitor when he went to court last year. Perhaps he was hoping for some kind of reward, but I think Father let slip how important the paper was and how the diary held the other part of the clue to the treasure, so Gott decided that he'd have the diary for himself."

"First he asked me for it nicely," Jamie remembered. "Then, when I said Rob had it, he assumed I meant in Rob's *house* and not at *work*. He robbed the house and didn't find it. That same evening he came round on some pretext about History research and had the cheek to ask for it!"

"He'll do anything to get it, Jamie. Anything. He's dangerous!"

"He's a fool," Jamie snorted. "Wouldn't dare hurt anyone."

"No. But his quiet, fat friend would."

"Podge?"

"Yes, Hodge . . . he has a knife."

"How do you know?"

Trish swallowed and looked nervously around. "I didn't finish telling you what happened this morning before I met you. I left home, still shaken from Father's fit of temper. Gott and his two friends were waiting for me as I walked past the graveyard. Said they wanted the diary. I told them I didn't have it. That you'd be returning it to Father tonight. Gott said he didn't want Father to have it. He said he wanted it for himself, or else . . ."

"Or else what?" Jamie said and he felt the anger rising in him.

"Or else they'd carve . . . they'd carve *you* up!" she murmured.

"They threaten you by saying they'd hurt me? Why?"

Trish fixed her gaze on the plastic table-top. "They have this idea that I . . . like you."

Suddenly thoughts of treasure were a million miles away from the boy. "And do you?" he asked clumsily, stupidly, regretting it as he said it.

"Of course not," Trish said quickly. Too quickly. "I mean . . ." she stumbled, confused. "Yes, I like you . . . enough to want you safe from Hodge's knife."

Jamie sighed. "And Hodge showed you the knife?"

She nodded and shuddered at the thought. "I'm scared. If I don't give them the diary they'll hurt you, and if I *do* give it to them then God knows what Father will do!" She shook her head. "What would you do?"

"I'd give your father the diary after we've had a look at this mysterious piece of paper. After all, the treasure does belong to him."

"You believe in treasure now?" she asked.

Jamie shook her head. "I feel I know a lot about Joshua Grey and his family now. The way Marie's going, I think she'll go off with John and be cut off from her family. That's why she isn't in the will. But something drastic must have happened to make Joshua bury his fortune. He seemed to love money so much." Jamie tapped the pile of paper that was Rob's last transcript. "You know he sent his sick daughter out in a boat on a cold October day just to pick up money for him! And he didn't care about the fact that she could be bringing cholera into Seawell . . . oh, hell! Joseph!"

"Who's he?" Trish asked.

"Oh, hell!" Jamie growled. "The stupid girl!"

"I thought you admired her," Trish said. One of her straight, black eyebrows was raised in amusement.

"Nobody's perfect," Jamie muttered. "When you're in love you do stupid things," he said.

Trish allowed her mouth to curl a little in a smile. "Speaking from experience?" she asked.

Jamie pulled a face. "Let's go."

Trish had to scramble to catch him at the door just as he collided with a teacher.

"Ah, there you are, Jamie. Hurry up – you're late!"

"Late, Mr Grint? What for?"

"For tonight's soccer match against Whitley. Don't say you've forgotten! Hurry up! Early kick-off so we're finished before dark!"

"Sorry, sir. Can't make it tonight!" he gasped and looked desperately at Trish.

"That's right, Mr Grint," Trish said, picking up her cue quickly. "He's going on a treasure hunt."

The teacher glared at her angrily. "You members of some kind of car club?"

"That's right, sir – Seawell Veteran and Vintage Club. We're marshalls!" she said quickly and bundled Jamie out into the cold evening.

"What's wrong, Jamie?" she asked as they hurried across the yard. "Didn't I come up with a good enough excuse?"

"It's not that," he said with a shake of the head. "It's just I never thought I'd see the day I'd find something more important than football!"

"A sign of growing up – changing your priorities," the girl explained.

"I think Marie was finding that," Jamie said.

They hurried through the darkening streets, Jamie explaining his plan as he went. "Rob should be back by now. We'll call at his house first and pick up the diary. See what this mysterious letter says, then deliver it to your father."

"And Eric Gott?" Trish asked.

"We'll devise something to keep him happy – some sort of fake, duplicate letter that'll keep him guessing for a year or two. Yes, the lights are on – Rob must be at home," he said as they turned the last corner. Then he stopped so suddenly that Trish collided with his shoulder.

"What's wrong?" she asked. She'd lowered her voice instinctively.

"Go back. Back round the corner," he answered softly.

He retreated and leaned against the end house. Carefully he peered round the corner again. "Eric Gott lives not far from Rob. You can see his house from here. The light was on in an upstairs window of his house. As we came round the corner I saw the curtain move."

"You think he's been waiting for us?"

"Yes. Now, we can make a run for our homes if you like – he'll never catch us," Jamie said.

"But we haven't got the diary or the paper from inside it," Trish said. "I daren't go home without it. And even if we get away this time we have to face them sooner or later!"

"Right. That's what I thought. So let's go ahead and see Rob, but when we leave we go in different directions. I'll take the diary. I'll carry it openly so they'll see it and follow me. But you take the paper –

that's the important thing your father's after. Get that to him."

"But what about you?" she asked, frowning.

"If necessary I'll give them the diary. It's not important, it never was. That should get them off our backs!" Jamie explained.

"They might hurt you," she said.

"I might hurt them," he replied with more boldness than he felt.

"My hero!" Trish said, with a grin that was only a little mocking. She squeezed his arm. Suddenly he did feel as brave as his words.

"Let's go!" he said.

He kept his eyes away from Gott's window and walked straight up to Rob's door as if he suspected nothing.

Rob answered. "Come in, Jamie . . . and you must be Trish? Pleased to meet you."

"Haven't time to stop, Rob. Can you just give us the diary – oh, and the paper you found pasted in the back – and we'll get it to Trish's father," Jamie said hurriedly.

"Oh, sure," Rob said. He disappeared into the house and came out a minute later with a bundle. He handed the items over separately. "There's the last transcript (make sure you're sitting down before you read it!), there's the original diary, and there's the pasted letter. As you see, I took it out to study it." Jamie passed it straight to Trish, who slipped it into her coat pocket. "Jamie says your father has the last sheet. I wonder what that says to make him think there's a buried fortune? He's a clever man, your father. Just single-minded. Needs to look at *all* the evidence he can. Has he looked in the parish register, for example?"

"I don't think so," Trish admitted.

"Tell him he should – he'll find lots of Treasures there!" he laughed.

"What do you mean?" Jamie asked and pulled up his collar against the cold wind.

"Come in and I'll explain," Rob said.

"No. We've got to get this over with, finally," Jamie said. "Just tell us."

"Very well. Joshua Grey married Caroline in 1812 – year of Napoleon's retreat from Moscow, you know . . ."

"I know, I know . . ." Jamie began impatiently.

"Well, if you know so much, tell me what Caroline's maiden name was!"

"How would I know that?"

"Same way I know it – looked it up in the parish register," Rob said smugly.

"So what is it?" Jamie asked, exasperated.

"Treasure. Caroline Treasure."

Jamie was perplexed for a moment. "So what? Surely that's not important!"

"Ah, Jamie, Jamie! What am I always telling you? Every clue may be important. Look at the parish register. What do you think your friend Marie's full name was? Eh?"

Jamie was shivering and becoming irritated by his brother's guessing games. "I don't know, but I can see you're going to enjoy telling me."

"Right! She was named after her mother. Marie Caroline *Treasure* Grey! And every oldest girl in the Grey family has had that family name ever since."

"I haven't," Trish argued.

"Haven't you?" Rob smiled.

"No. I'm just plain Tricia Grey."

"Because someone in the 1920s decided Tricia was more fashionable than Treasure, Treasure became Tricia. Tricia – Treasure. Same difference. You are the present Treasure of Grey Manor!" Rob laughed.

Jamie turned on his heel. "Come on, Treasure – we've got another kind of Treasure to find. Goodnight, Rob! See you later – we'll prove you wrong."

Rob roared with laughter. "I'll never make a historian out of you, Jamie! You've got your theory and now you're out to prove it. Remember the flat Earth people!" he called after his brother as he retreated along the road.

"What was that about flat Earth?" Trish asked.

"Oh, nothing. Just my brother's so used to being right he can't bear the thought that he might be wrong in this case," Jamie said, annoyed.

They stopped on the street corner. Jamie turned to face the girl. Her face was a pale, beautiful mask in the darkening air. "OK? You go that way and I'll go this. See you back at your house. Don't look now, but someone's just opened Gott's door a little and they're watching us."

"Good luck, Jamie," she said. She leaned forward a little so the sweet smell of her hair washed over him.

"Let's give them something to watch," she said and kissed him on the cheek before turning and walking briskly down the street.

Jamie rubbed his cheek, bewildered, and had to stop himself from running after her. Feeling a little dazed he set off in the opposite direction.

Someone was following him, that was certain. But they made no attempt to catch him up even though the diary was in his hand. What would happen, he wondered, if he reached Grey Manor and still had the diary? The plan would have failed.

The wind had dropped and the mist was rolling in from the river as he reached the end of Manor Walk. He could scarcely walk any slower. He made a sudden decision. He walked through the gates of the graveyard.

He walked up to the marble tomb of the Grey Family. He scanned the names of Joshua, died 1835, Caroline, died 1835 . . . then Marie Caroline Treasure Grey. The inscription read, 'Here lies our Treasure'.

Then he saw the date. "Oh, no!" he moaned softly. "Oh, no! Not that!"

And a voice behind him said, "Right, Williams! Hand over that diary – now!"

Chapter Ten

Jamie stared at the tombstone and tried to work out what had happened. He knew the answer lay in the transcript in his pocket, but it was hard to concentrate on the details with three boys breathing down his neck.

"You going to give me that diary or do I have to tell Podge to use his little carver on your face?" Gott rasped.

Jamie didn't turn round. He just threw the diary tiredly to the gravel path. He heard them scrambling as they fought over it. At last Gott's voice gave a cry of disgust. "It isn't here! It isn't flaming here!"

Jamie felt his shoulder grabbed roughly as he was swung round to face them. "Where is it?" Gott asked.

"Yeah! Tell us, or else!" Shorty said and brought his spotty face close to Jamie's.

Podge stayed expressionless and silent as ever but his hand slipped menacingly into his jacket pocket.

"It's safely in Mr Grey's hands," Jamie said quietly.

"You gave it to that old goat! He'll get the treasure! You stupid . . . you could have had a share. He reckons it'd be worth millions at today's values. Now the miser won't give us a penny!" Gott raged.

Jamie gestured over his shoulder. "There's your treasure – under that gravestone," he said simply.

Gott's mouth fell open. "Read it, Shorty! What's it say?"

The tall boy followed the words with a finger, mumbling until he reached the last line. "Here!" he cried. "Look at this! It says, 'Here lies our treasure'!"

Gott gave a whoop of joy and punched the unmoving Podge on the shoulder. "Under this gravestone all the time! Go and get the tools out of the hut, Podge. We might as well get it now before old Grey turns up!"

"What?" Shorty gasped. "You're not digging up a grave, Rick? You can't do that!"

"Shut up, Shorty! There'll be nothing there but dust after all this time. No bodies – just dust and treasure!" Gott gloated.

Jamie stepped forward.

"No! You're not disturbing her. Not Marie! You don't understand . . ."

"Podge!" Gott ordered sharply. "Get Williams and lock him in the hut."

Jamie should have used the slow response time of Podge to get a start on the fat boy. Instead he wasted it arguing. "You're making a horrible mistake . . . there's no fortune there . . ."

Podge grabbed him and pinned his arms behind his back. Jamie struggled and was amazed at the boy's strength. He was almost lifted off his feet and practically thrown towards the old stone hut in the middle of the graveyard. The door was open. Podge flung him across the floor and Jamie crashed into the far wall. A projection on the rough stone caught the side of his head. He struggled to his feet, dazed and sickened as blood flowed from a gash on his temple.

A candle lit the room, and though his vision was blurred he could make out the glint of the knife thrust in front of his face. He swayed towards it. "Careful, Podge, we don't want to carve him just yet. See if what he says about the treasure is true. If we dig that grave and find it's empty then you can rearrange his face, I promise."

Jamie shook his head to try and clear it. That was a mistake. It simply made him feel faint with pain. He leaned back against the cool stone wall.

"Know what this place is, Mister clever historian?" Gott sneered. Jamie closed his eyes so the hut would stop spinning round and didn't answer. "We did our research well, didn't we, boys?"

Somewhere in the greyness Jamie heard Shorty snigger. "Yeah, Rick. This is a watchman's hut. Built in the eighteen-twenties so the relatives of the corpses could keep a watch; guard against the body-snatchers!" he explained proudly.

"That's right," Gott crooned. "And do you know what it's built from?" he asked.

Somehow Jamie managed to form a word. It was slurred and drunken. "Shtone!"

"Yeah. Stone, but not just any old stone. It's built of old gravestones! Nice touch that, isn't it? The council uses it now to keep their tools in. Handy, that. Shorty! Grab that shovel. Podge! There's a crowbar. Grab it. I'll take this tarpaulin. Know what that's for, Williams? It's to put the soil on as we shovel it out. Makes it easier to put back later and leave the area looking undisturbed. Old body-snatcher's trick, that. Told you we'd done our homework well, didn't I?" he laughed.

Jamie heard the boys moving towards the door. "Oh, Williams, don't try shouting – these gravestone walls are thick. And don't try getting out the door. The bolt's as thick as Podge's wrist." Jamie forced his eyes open enough to see the door slam shut. He let himself sink to the floor.

His fingers explored his forehead. The blood had slowed to a trickle but it was running into his eye. He used his handkerchief to staunch the flow. He wasn't sure how long he sat there before his head began to clear enough for him to take in the situation.

The walls were indeed solid. His fingers ran over the stones and to his horror he realised that the scratches on the stone spelled out names of long-dead people. The floor was paved stone and the door massively solid oak. The windows in the side had been bricked up some years ago. None of the tools left in the hut – rakes, grass-clippers and trowels – promised to help him escape from this grim prison.

Jamie sat at the rough wooden bench, leaned on the table and rested his head on his hands. The cut seemed to be opening again so he reached into his pocket for the handkerchief. Instead he felt a thick wad of paper and pulled out Rob's last transcript of Marie's diary.

With nothing else to do he squinted at the pages in the poor light of the candle and was jolted back in time a hundred and fifty years.

I write this by the light of a farthing candle. I am in the poorhouse hospital. Not because I'm poor, and not because I'm sick, although the fever of my chill is no better and my coughing makes my body ache.

It does not matter. For there are people here who have suffered more and will suffer again if I can't help them.

I first came here to visit Joseph. Molly said that Billy's friend from the ship was ill and in the hospital. We went together to the quayside. The hospital was guarded by some grim matron.

"What do you want?" she asked abruptly.

"I am Marie Grey of Grey Manor," I said, undaunted by this griffin. "I believe you have a sailor here – his name is Joseph. We wish to visit him."

"Then do so at your own risk," the woman said sourly.

127

"What risk?" I asked.

Her ugly face turned bitter. "The risk of cholera," she said. "For cholera it is that ails him. And some fool women brought him from that ship beyond the harbour to spread disease through Seawell. Not risk to their own kind, of course! No risk to the rich of Seawell – only risk to the people of the quayside and we who have to care for him."

I would have answered her but Molly silenced me with a tug on my sleeve. "But may we see him, Mrs Robson?" she asked.

The matron looked at my maid sternly. "Very well, Molly Brown, as he is your brother's friend. But you must wait until his relatives have left the bed-side."

"Relatives?" Molly said. "But Joseph is a Dutch-man. Captain Carter picked him up at some French port on the outward journey two years ago. He cannot have relatives in Seawell."

Mrs Robson's granite face dissolved in fear. "Come in, Molly," she said and led us into the low building. It was clean and well-swept but the smell of sickness filled the air. Small windows let in little light and not a breath of air. A row of beds ran down each wall. A door led to another room. Mrs Robson nodded at it, "We keep the cholera victims through there – try to stop its spread as best we can." She sat down at a table and invited us to sit there too. Some poor soul moaned a cry for help and then fell silent.

"Who are these relatives?" I asked.

The matron looked at me with sharp, black eyes. "If

what you say is true then I fear they may be sack-'em-up men come to ply their trade."

"Body-snatchers!" Molly gasped. "But Joseph isn't dead!"

"I've heard this tale from other poorhouse keepers," the matron said. "You know that if a pauper dies the council must pay for the funeral . . ." I didn't know, but nodded anyway. "The council is glad to see the family claim the body and save them the cost of a funeral. So sack-'em-ups discovered that if they found some dying, lonely person it was easy to claim them. When the pauper dies the sack-'em-ups take the body and they sell straight to the surgeons – saves the trouble of them digging up a grave."

"And that's what's happening to Joseph now?" I cried. "We have to stop them!" and I hurried to the door. I swung it open. The hospital smelled bad, but the stench from the cholera room churned my feeble stomach. Joseph lay pale and weakly groaning on the bed, muttering in some language that I didn't know.

Two men in rough brown clothes were laughing loud and drinking from a stone jar. They swung to face me. One bared yellow teeth at me in an evil grin. "Ah, Miss," he croaked. "Joseph was just telling us one of his jokes . . ." he tried to lie.

"Get out!" I told him.

The smile slid from his face. "We have the right to visit our dying uncle," he snarled.

"He's not your uncle," I said. His watery eyes were bloodshot and filled with hate for me. Even through the smell of sickness in the room I felt I could sense the smell of death that hung around him – the same smell I'd smelled that night I'd visited John and been pursued by the body-snatchers.

His friend was smaller with a face that a rat would be ashamed to own. "What makes you think that he isn't our uncle?" he whined.

"I know he is not because he's my uncle," I said as calmly as I could, though I'll swear I was trembling fit to shake the poorhouse down.

The rat-faced one looked at the one with yellow teeth. "Perhaps we made a mistake, friend . . . he looks a lot like our Uncle Joseph . . . but we could be mistaken."

They began to edge towards the door. I wanted to turn and run but something kept me there. "One more thing," I said. "I will be paying for his funeral . . . and I shall make sure his body is well guarded. You shan't have him after his death, either!"

I thought, from his expression, that Yellow-Teeth was going to spring for my throat. He was panting as he neared me, his stinking breath making me sick. "Beware, my beauty!" he hissed. "If we are cheated of Joseph perhaps we'll find some compensation elsewhere. You don't look long for this world yourself, Miss. And for a fine specimen like yourself the surgeons would pay us twenty guineas! It will be my pleasure to hand you over!"

I swayed back, faint against the doorpost as he shouldered his way past me and the body-snatchers fled.

"Oh, Miss, what have you done?" Molly breathed.

"She's defeated them, that's what," the matron

130

said. And I thought I saw respect begin to replace contempt in her face.

"I meant what I said about Joseph," I said. "We will pay for a decent funeral if . . . when he dies."

The man moaned again. Mrs Robson took a cloth from a bowl of water and wiped it over his fevered brow. From the main room a woman cried in pain. The matron called, "I'll be with you soon."

"Here, give me the rag," I said. I took over the bathing of Joseph's forehead while Mrs Robson tended the other cases. Molly began to help with sweeping and at noon began cooking a meal of gruel for those who were well enough to eat. I could not touch the food myself.

Some time in the afternoon Joseph died.

I sent Molly to make arrangements for the funeral and went on tending the other sick in the hospital. "Don't we need a doctor to help?" I asked.

Mrs Robson shook her head. "We are given the building. The charity allows us a little money for food, but doctors cost far too much for the likes of us."

No sooner had poor Molly returned from the undertaker than I sent her off to find Doctor Flint and promised to pay from my clothes allowance.

But before the old doctor arrived a more unexpected visitor came.

"What are you doing here?" he asked sternly.

"Oh, Father!" I said. "How good to see you. You must see how these poor people live . . ." but Papa didn't want to listen.

"Go home, Marie," he said.

"But Father," I argued, "these people need help."

"Then let them help themselves," he said. "Go home."

I have often teased my father till I get my own way, but I have never openly defied him before. "Father, I cannot go home. I could not return to live in the comforts of Grey Manor while these poor people live like this."

Papa's face was red. A vein throbbed in his temple. I thought he was going to strike me. "Go home, child . . . now!"

I looked at him, a child no longer. "Father, I love you . . . and I believed you love me too. If you do, then let me stay."

He shook his head, bewildered and weakening. "Young ladies of our class do not work in poorhouses. If you want to do good, join Mrs Fawcett's group. Raise money. Distribute Bibles. But you do not have to dirty your own hands."

"I do, Father. You can see the problem from where you stand, but you cannot understand it until you dirty your hands. I saw a man die this afternoon, Father."

"You shouldn't have to . . ." he said.

"I may not ever have to again if we can stop them dying. But if his cholera spreads then I'm to blame. I brought him ashore. Do you know they cannot afford doctors here?"

"I'll pay for the doctors," he offered suddenly.

"Thank you, Father," I said and put my arms around his neck to give a hug of thanks.

"I will send for doctors . . . when you return to Grey Manor."

I sighed. "Tomorrow, Father. Mrs Robson needs a

rest. I promised to stay the night and let her go home."

"You are a stubborn young lady," he said severely.

"And spoilt," I reminded him.

That brought a small smile to his stern face. "And spoilt."

"I think I get my stubborn character from you, Father."

I think that pleased rather than annoyed him. "Yes. You are a true Grey!" he said and turned and walked stiffly away. "I want you back in Grey Manor tomorrow morning. We'll talk about what we can do then. I don't know what your mother will think."

"You can persuade her that people are more important than jewels," I said.

"I'll try," he promised. "Goodnight, Treasure!"

"Goodnight, Papa!"

Molly returned soon after. "Oh, it's so cold tonight," she complained. "They haven't any fuel here to light a fire."

"Something else I can arrange tomorrow," I said.

"Doctor Flint's here now," she said.

The old man came in and spent an hour here. He prescribed medicines and treatment for all the patients then he took me to the matron's room at the back. "They'll all survive to face another day," he promised.

"That's good," I sighed.

He looked at me gravely then said, "It is you I worry about."

"I'm fine. I'm just a little tired," I said.

"You're ill," he said. "You've always had weak lungs. That chill had made them worse before you took *that foolish trip out on a freezing river! And now you have a fever. The only cure is rest and warmth, but instead you've chosen work and cold. Your body cannot stand much more . . ."*

"I'm young," I smiled.

"Too young to die," he said harshly.

"I've already promised Father that I'll return to Grey Manor tomorrow and rest," I explained.

"I hope you live to see tomorrow," he said cruelly. "Stay in this room. Rest. Stay warm. At least do that," he said.

"I would but the patients might need my care," I told him.

"Molly can do that. Now rest," he said firmly and left.

And Molly has been good. She brought my diary and quills. I cannot sleep. My body is aching too much. Perhaps I worked too hard for one not used to such work.

Still, Molly has promised that John will come round later tonight when he finishes work.

To think! John in this small room with me . . . and no chaperone! The Old Besom would have palpitations!

Tonight, I am determined, John shall not be permitted to call me Miss Grey! He shall call me Marie. I am Marie Caroline Treasure and Marie he shall call me!

Molly has gone to fetch him now. I am wearing my favourite blue cotton dress – the deep blue I know that matches my eyes. Even by the light of a farthing candle I shall be beautiful for John.

Foolish Molly refused to damp my dress with water. Said that the night's too cold. I cannot feel it cold. I feel

I am burning. If I soak my dress in water it can only cool me.

John will love me, and he will call me Marie.

[The diary of Marie ends here. Perhaps I was wrong, Jamie, and the middle class aren't all bad. Perhaps there's no such thing as a class. Perhaps there are just people – good people and bad people. Marie was vain and foolish and generous and brave. Two hundred people died in that cholera epidemic in 1831, thanks to Marie Grey's rashness. But then we'll never count the thousands who were saved by the Grey money that was spent to improve the lot of the poor in Seawell, thanks to Marie Grey's caring. I should have said that the diary *as written by Marie* ends here. There was a carefully written note after the last entry in another hand. I thought you might like to read it –Rob.]

My name is John Brown. Tonight I came to the poor-house to help Miss Grey. I found her in the matron's room. Her head rested on the table. I didn't want to wake her but she stirred and looked up.

Her face was pale as death, yet as she tried to rise I caught her and she was hot as coals. I laid her on the bench and held her hand. Somehow her dress was soaked in water and the cold of the poorhouse was killing her.

I called my sister to fetch blankets. But Miss Grey stopped me. "Hold me, John," she said. I wrapped my arms around her thin, damp body and felt her frail breathing grow weaker. "Miss Grey, you must let me take you back to Grey Manor."

She shook her head and said something so faintly that I had to put my ear next to her lips to catch it. "What was that, Miss Grey?" I asked.

"Call me Marie," she whispered.

"Marie. Let me take you home, Marie."

Her deep blue eyes looked at me and she smiled. "I knew I'd make you call me Marie," she sighed. Then her eyes seemed to look through me to some other world beyond this one. And so Marie Grey died in my arms.

I cannot read this diary in her secret writing. But if some future day someone can understand I tell you this. Marie was a Grey by name but in spirit she was fit to be a daughter of Low Street.

'And that was the greatest tribute John Brown could pay her – Rob.]

Chapter Eleven

Jamie felt more sickened by the final page of the diary than by the aching in his head.

Then his stomach tightened to think of Gott and his gang despoiling the grave outside. He rose shakily and tried the door. It was solid as the gravestone walls, but he could hear something – shouting and a scuffling over the gravel.

Footsteps. Running. Towards the hut!

The bolt rattled and he stepped back just in time as the door swung open. He tried to collect his dazed mind for an escape. But when he saw the man in the doorway he stopped.

"Mr Grey!" he cried. "Did Trish tell you that I . . ."

But Edward Grey wasn't listening. His eyes were

wild as Jamie had seen them once before. He held a pointed spade in one hand and a torch in the other. Behind him stood Eric Gott – face red with the exertion of digging and muddied with earth.

"It isn't there, Mr Grey . . . we've dug for nearly an hour! Williams lied to us. We'll kill him!"

"He didn't lie to you . . . he was nearly right," the man said. "Trouble is, he didn't have that last sheet."

"So where is it?" Gott asked.

Trish's father struck the paved floor of the hut with the spade. The ringing echoed in the hut then died in the foggy night. "It's here!" he said. "Under this floor."

"Aw, no!" Shorty moaned. "To think we've hung round here for a week and never knew it was under our feet all the time."

"We'll dig it out now," Gott said. "Podge! Start digging."

Mr Grey swung round. "I don't need the help of you young ruffians," he snarled. "Get out!" He hardly noticed Jamie watching carefully from the corner.

Gott stepped back. "Podge," he said nastily, "the gentleman doesn't want to co-operate. Show him your carver and persuade him!"

Podge stepped forward and drew his knife. The man's spade had been resting on the floor. Suddenly he swept it upwards and smashed knife and Podge's hand at a stroke. The fat boy had scarcely time to run off howling into the mist before Mr Grey rushed forward and brought the spade back down. The flat of the spade caught Eric Gott a sickening crack on the side of his head. He fell like a sack of bones and lay still. Shorty didn't wait to see what the man would do next. He ran into the night.

Jamie watched in horror as Mr Grey put the point of the spade into a crack in the paving and began to lift it. "Don't stand here, boy!" he ordered. "Get a grip on the stone as I lift – help me!"

Jamie shook his head numbly and edged past the man. While the spade was jammed in the paving he felt safe.

He rounded the sweating, cursing man, stepped over the lifeless Gott, and reached the door. He staggered out into the night. And he collided with the first of the policemen to arrive on the scene. While the police entered the hut and struggled to arrest Mr Grey Jamie wandered to the gates of the graveyard.

The light spilling from the phonebox showed Trish standing, watching. She moved and they met in the middle of the cobbled walk.

"Oh, Jamie!" she breathed. "I think he's mad. He's finally gone mad!" She peered at him in the faint light. "Your head! All that blood! Did he do that?"

Jamie shook his head weakly. "Gott," he managed to say.

"Oh, Jamie," she said. She reached forward and held him. And when the police led her handcuffed father out to the waiting car she buried her head in his shoulder so she wouldn't have to see him.

"Was it you who phoned us?" a policeman asked.

She nodded.

"Would you like to come to the station and answer a few questions? And you'd better have that knock on the head seen to, young man," he added. "Could I have your names?"

After giving them Jamie said, "Couldn't we come to the police station tomorrow? We need to find somewhere for Trish to stay this evening. She can't go back to Grey Manor."

"I'll go to my mother's house," she said. "I've a feeling I'll be staying there a lot more in the future."

"OK," the policeman nodded. "Seawell police station tomorrow morning. Nine o'clock. Need a lift, young lady?"

"Thanks," she said.

"And you'd better come with me to hospital, young man," the policeman insisted.

Jamie followed him to a waiting car.

He sat in the back with Trish. Comfortingly close. "What happened after I left? And why did your father try to dig up the hut floor?" he asked.

They had reached the house where Trish's mother lived. "Tomorrow, Jamie. We'll sort it all out tomorrow."

The girl opened the car door, then impulsively leaned back into the car and, for the second time that evening, kissed him on the cheek. "See you at the police station tomorrow morning – then we'll meet at Rob's and try to piece it all together."

"Goodnight, Jamie."

"Goodnight, Treasure."

"I told father that Marie was really the Treasure of Grey Manor," Trish explained as she sipped Rob's coffee the next morning. "But he was still convinced that it was just a cover for the burial of some real treasure. Even when he read the first part of the missing letter he didn't take it all in."

Rob nodded. "He saw in the evidence what he wanted to see. Bad historian, I'm afraid."

"I still haven't seen this letter," Jamie objected. "You two have. What does it say?"

"The police have the original, but I made a copy," Rob said, sifting through the sheets in his briefcase. "Here it is. It was written by Joshua Grey. Someone must have been arranging the material in Grey Manor at some time and decided it fitted on Marie's diary. They pasted it in. And, of course, Eric Gott found the second sheet."

Jamie read it carefully.

Our Daughter, Marie, has died. I do not yet fully understand why she died. Of course I know that her disease was pneumonia, I mean I don't understand why she placed herself in such danger. But I must try to understand what she wanted. I must try to give her what she wants – wanted – or her death will have been futile.

The last time I saw her, the last thing she said, was something about people being more important than money. Dear God, I see the truth in that! For all my money cannot buy back Marie now.

My Treasure was worth more than all my treasure.

So all my treasure must be used to save the lives of others that she loved. At the funeral the vicar said, 'It is easier for a camel to go through the eye of a needle than for a rich man to enter the kingdom of God.' I am ashamed to say that I wept, for he went on to read another verse of that chapter; he said, 'Thou shalt have treasure in heaven.'

So, if I am to join my Treasure in heaven, I must give away all that I earn or use it in some good cause.

Already I have made plans for my builders to knock down Low Street and build proper houses for my workers and their families. Then I shall pay those workers a decent wage and provide for their old age with a comfortable poorhouse.

Jamie looked up. "So that's what happened to the Grey fortune! He didn't gamble it away or lose it through the Seawell cholera quarantine, he simply gave it away. Why didn't we think of that?"

"Because it seemed so out of character for Joshua Grey – the man we met at the start of Marie's diary," Trish explained.

"So why did your father still believe in the treasure? If he read this he must have seen where it went," Jamie argued.

"What did Marie say in her last entry? You can see something but not understand it until you've been there," Rob said. "Trish's father could *see* what Marie's grieving father wrote but he's never experienced the loss of a daughter so he couldn't *understand* what it did to the man. He didn't believe that the treasure was gone – and, more important, he didn't *want* to believe it."

"And where did he get the idea that the treasure was buried in the hut?" Jamie asked, absently fingering the bandage on his head.

Rob drained his coffee cup and nodded at the paper on the table. "Read the rest of that letter. The *real* reason he wrote it was to tell his descendants where Marie was buried, so they could honour the grave of the girl who changed the history of Seawell."

Jamie was puzzled. "But we know where Marie was buried. In the same grave as her father and mother."

"That's what Eric Gott thought too," Trish said. "Even if there were jewels buried with Marie then they weren't in that place. Finish reading the letter," she urged.

Jamie turned to the next page.

On the day of Marie's funeral I turned to my Bible for comfort. I tried to find St Matthew's comforting words about finding Treasure in heaven. But instead I found Chapter 24 and my blood curdled as I read verse 28: 'Wheresoever the carcase is, there will the eagles be gathered together.'

And I remembered something Marie's maid had babbled in her grief – that there were body-snatchers in the area. Somehow she had the idea that they were out to disturb my daughter's peace with their evil activities.

And so I devised a plan to thwart them. We placed the unclaimed body of a sailor in a coffin – a Dutchman called Joseph, I believe. We buried it in the Grey vault in public with a grand service. If the body-snatchers were watching then I hope our deception will spoil their plans.

In the middle of the graveyard there is a small hut. It was built as a watch hut for the sexton. It has a strong door and walls. In there it is as safe as Grey Manor. As darkness fell, we raised the stone floor and placed the coffin with our real Treasure beneath . . ."

The page ended. Jamie looked up. Trish quietly repeated the words of the last page. The page that Eric Gott had found and handed to her father.

"And that is where we buried our Treasure tonight. Safe from the evil, grasping hands that would desecrate the most perfect Treasure any family ever had. Dated the first day of November in the year of our Lord Eighteen hundred and thirty-one."

The three sat silently for a few minutes. Finally Rob spoke. "Just one year later a change in the law released all unclaimed bodies to the surgeons for experiments, free of charge. They provided all that the surgeons needed. And the trade of body-snatching was killed at a stroke.

"And four years later Joshua and Caroline Grey died. The archives show that he gave half a million pounds to local charities, but he was broken man. Lost a lot of interest in his work. He promoted a young man to look after the shipping side of his business – caused a bit of a stir at the time but he became a great success. The young man's name was quite a common one – John Brown. By 1835 Joshua Grey had virtually retired to live a simple life in Grey Manor. His wife died at Easter that year and he followed shortly after. The house went to Louise Grey's husband in the will.''

"I remember the will!" Jamie said. "Trish's father read part of it to us. It didn't make a lot of sense at the time . . . what was it again, Trish?"

"My Treasure is buried," she quoted. *"By the time you read this I shall be buried too. I trust that my wealth may bring peace and happiness to others in the future, a happiness it never brought to me."*

"And your father thought he was the future that Joshua was referring to," Jamie said sadly. He turned to his brother. "Have you heard what's going to happen to Mr Grey?"

"The police were round earlier today to say they'd checked the fingerprints on the back door and they matched with Gott's," Rob said. "I asked them about your father, Trish. I don't know if it's for me to tell you what they said."

"Please," the girl said. "I'd rather hear it from you."

"They said he's to be charged with assault on Gott. He fractured the boy's skull, but it must be extra thick because they reckon he'll recover," Rob said grimly. "And when young Gott wakes up he'll find a policeman waiting to charge him with burglary at this house and desecrating the churchyard. I don't think he'll be going back to Seawell Comprehensive to trouble you again, Jamie. Hodge is in trouble for carrying an offensive weapon and I think Short will be implicated."

"Then you don't know the worst," Trish said. "My father needed money for something else," she went on slowly. "You see, he couldn't afford to run Grey Manor on his wage as a clerk . . ."

"I thought he was a lawyer," Jamie said.

Trish shook her head. "He liked to tell people that. He failed his law exams because he spent too much time studying History instead. Became a solicitor's clerk. Anyway, he made up his wage shortage by embezzling the firm's money, but after getting away with it for ten years they were catching up with him. He was desperate for at least forty thousand pounds. He had to pay back the money or go to prison. The treasure was his only hope. I think he'll be locked away for a long time."

"And you?" Jamie asked.

"I'll stay with my mother. I'll be happier there. I always tried to be loyal to him – I owed him that – but I hated living in that house with all its ghosts," she shivered. "I couldn't live a normal life like the other girls. He discouraged friends coming round. That's how I got a reputation in school for being . . . well, a bit odd. A snob."

"Sorry," Jamie murmured guiltily.

"What will happen to Grey Manor?" Rob asked.

"I think they'll sell it to pay off the money Father stole by fraud."

"Ahh! In that case I think I know a buyer."

"You?" Jamie asked.

"No!" Rob laughed. "The Seawell History Society has a grant to buy a museum and they've been looking for a suitable building. I believe I've just found them one."

Jamie was thoughtful for a long while. At last he said, "Rob?"

"Mmm?"

"In these museums don't they have guidebooks?"

"Of course – to explain the artefacts to the visitors."

"I'd like to write one," he offered, then looked shyly at the girl beside him. "If Trish would help me."

"Her picture's on the wall," she said softly. "She looks beautiful but . . . but her real beauty was in her nature. Someone *should* write her story."

"I couldn't do it without your help," Jamie said earnestly.

"And I wouldn't let you!" Trish said with a smile. "She was the first Treasure of Grey Manor – it's only fair that the last Treasure of Grey Manor should have her say."

GREEN WATCH

GREEN WATCH is a new series of fast moving environmental thrillers, in which a group of young people battle against the odds to save the natural world from ruthless exploitation. All titles are printed on recycled paper.

BATTLE FOR THE BADGERS by Anthony Masters
Tim's world has been turned upside down. His dad's in prison, his mum's had a breakdown, and he's been sent to stay with his weird Uncle Seb. Seb and his two Kids, Flower and Brian, run Green Watch – a pressure group that supports green issues. At first Tim thinks they're a bunch of cranks – but soon he finds himself entangled in a fervent battle to save badgers from needless extermination . . .

SAD SONG OF THE WHALE by Anthony Masters
Tim leaps at the chance to join Green Watch on an anti-whaling expedition in the Falklands. However, events don't turn out quite as he expected. And soon, he and the other members of Green Watch, find themselves shipwrecked and fighting for their lives . . .

Look out for these forthcoming titles in the GREEN WATCH series:

Dolphin's Revenge by Anthony Masters
Monsters On The Beach by Anthony Masters

PRESS GANG

Why not pick up one of the PRESS GANG books, and follow the adventures of the teenagers who work on the *Junior Gazette*? Based on the original TV series produced for Central Television.

Book 1: First Edition
As editor of the brand new *Junior Gazette*, and with five days to get the first edition on the street, the last thing Lynda needs is more problems. Then an American called Spike strolls into her newsroom and announces he's been made a member of the *Gazette* team too . . .

Book 2: Public Exposure
Lynda is delighted when the *Junior Gazette* wins a computer in a writing competition. But she can't help feeling that it was all a little too easy . . . Then articles for the *Gazette* start to appear mysteriously on the computer screen. Who is the mystery writer, and why won't he reveal his identity?

Book 3: Checkmate
It's midnight, and Lynda's got to put together a whole new edition of the *Junior Gazette* by morning. The only way she can do it is to lock the office, keeping her staff in and their parents out! Spike's supposed to be taking a glamorous new date to a party – how is he going to react to being locked in the newsroom for the night?

Book 4: The Date
It's going to be a big evening for Lynda – a cocktail party where she'll be introduced to lots of big names in the newspaper business. There's only one problem: who's going to be her date? The answer's obvious to most of the *Junior Gazette* team, but Lynda is determined that the last person she'll take to the party is Spike Thomson!

MYSTERY THRILLER

Introducing, a new series of hard hitting, action packed thrillers for young adults.

THE SONG OF THE DEAD by Anthony Masters
For the first time in years 'the song of the dead' is heard around the mud flats of Whitstable. But this time is it really the ghostly cries of dead sailors? Or is it something far more sinister? Barney Hampton is sure that something strange is going on – and he's determined to get to the bottom of the mystery . . .

THE FERRYMAN'S SON by Ian Strachan
Rob is convinced that Drewe and Miles are up to no good. Why else would two sleek city whizz-kids want to spend the summer yachting around a sleepy Devonshire village? Where do they go on their frequent night cruises? And why does the lovely Kimberley go with them? Then Kimberley disappears, and Rob finds himself embroiled in a web of deadly intrigue . . .

Further titles to look out for in the Mystery Thriller series:

Treasure of Grey Manor by Terry Deary
The Foggiest by Dave Belbin
Blue Murder by Jay Kelso
Dead Man's Secret by Linda Allen
Fighting Back by Peter Beere